GW00976326

# Dot & the Kangaroo

*The Kangaroo finds Dot*

# Dot & the Kangaroo

BY ETHEL PEDLEY

*illustrated by*
FRANK MAHONY

An imprint of HarperCollins*Publishers*

*Publisher's Note*

The illustrations in this edition have been made from the orginals of the Frank Mahony drawings that appeared in the first edition of 1899. They are reproduced by courtesy of the Trustees of the Mitchell Library.

*AN ANGUS & ROBERTSON BOOK*
*An imprint of HarperCollinsPublishers*

*First published in 1899*
*First published in Australia in 1906 by Angus & Robertson Publishers*
*New edition 1965, reprinted nine times*
*Commemorative edition 1986, reprinted 1989*
*This edition first published in Australia in 1991 by*
*CollinsAngus&Robertson Publishers Pty Limited (ACN 009 913 517)*
*A division of HarperCollinsPublishers (Australia) Pty Limited*
*4 Eden Park, 31 Waterloo Road, North Ryde, NSW 2113, Australia*

*William Collins Publishers Ltd*
*31 View Road, Glenfield, Auckland 10, New Zealand*

*HarperCollinsPublishers Limited*
*77-85 Fulham Palace Road, London W6 8JB, United Kingdom*



*National Library of Australia*
*Cataloguing-in-Publication data:*

*Pedley, Ethel.*
*Dot and the kangaroo.*

*ISBN 0 207 17338 9*
*I. Kangaroos — Juvenile fiction. I. Title.*

*A823'.2.*

*Cover illustration by Margaret Power*
*Printed in Australia by Griffin Press Limited*

*5 4 3 2 1*
*95 94 93 92 91*

*To the*
*children of Australia*
*in the hope of enlisting their sympathies*
*for the many*
*beautiful, amiable, and frolicsome creatures*
*of their fair land,*
*whose extinction, through ruthless destruction,*
*is being surely accomplished*

# Chapter One

LITTLE Dot had lost her way in the bush. She knew it, and was very frightened. She was too frightened in fact to cry, but stood in the middle of a little dry, bare space, looking around her at the scraggy growths of prickly shrubs that had torn her little dress to rags, scratched her bare legs and feet till they bled, and pricked her hands and arms as she had pushed madly through the bushes, for hours, seeking her home. Sometimes she looked up to the sky. But little of it could be seen because of the great tall trees that seemed to her to be trying to reach heaven with their far-off crooked branches. She could see little patches of blue sky between the tangled tufts of drooping leaves, and, as the dazzling sunlight had faded, she began to think it was getting late, and that very soon it would be night.

The thought of being lost and alone in the wild bush at night took her breath away with fear, and made her tired little legs tremble under her. She gave up all hope of finding her home, and sat down at the foot of the biggest blackbutt tree, with her face buried in her hands and knees, and thought of all that had happened, and what might happen yet.

It seemed such a long, long time since her mother had told her that she might gather some bush flowers whilst she cooked the dinner, and Dot recollected how she was bid not to go out of sight of the cottage. How she wished now that she had remembered this sooner! But while she was picking the pretty flowers, a hare suddenly started at her feet and sprang away into the bush, and she had run after it.

When she found that she could not catch the hare, she discovered that she could no longer see the cottage. After wandering for a while she got frightened and ran, and ran, little knowing that she was going farther away from her home at every step.

Where she was sitting under the blackbutt tree, she was miles away from her father's selection, and it would be very difficult for anyone to find her. She felt that she was a long way off, and she began to think of what was happening at home. She remembered how, not very long ago, a neighbour's little boy had been lost, and how his mother had come to their cottage for help to find him, and that her father had ridden off on the big bay horse to bring men from all the selections around to help in the search. She remembered their coming back in the darkness; numbers of strange men she had never seen before. Old men, young men, and boys, all on their rough-coated horses, and how they came indoors, and what a noise they made all talking together in their big deep voices. They looked terrible men, so tall and brown and fierce, with their rough bristly beards; and they all spoke in such funny tones to her, as if they were trying to make their voices small.

During many days these men came and went, and every time they were more sad and less noisy. The little boy's mother used to come and stay, crying, whilst the men were searching the bush for her little son. Then, one evening, Dot's father came home alone, and both her mother and the little boy's mother went away in a great hurry. Then, very late, her mother came back crying, and her father sat smoking by the fire, looking very sad, and she never saw that little boy again, although he had been found.

She wondered now if all these rough, big men were riding into the bush to find her, and if, after many days, they would find her, and no one ever see her again. She seemed to see her mother crying, and her father very sad, and all the men very solemn. These thoughts made her so miserable that she began to cry herself.

Dot does not know how long she was sobbing in loneliness and fear, with her head on her knees, and with her little hands covering her eyes so as not to see the cruel wild bush in which she was lost. It seemed a long time before she summoned up courage to uncover her weeping eyes, and look once more at the bare, dry earth, and the wilderness of scrub and trees that seemed to close her in as if she were in a prison. When she did look up, she was surprised to see that she was no longer alone. She forgot all her trouble and fear in her astonishment at seeing a big grey Kangaroo squatting quite close to her, in front of her.

What was most surprising was that the Kangaroo evidently understood that Dot was in trouble, and was sorry for her; for down the animal's nice soft grey muzzle two tiny little tears were slowly trickling. When Dot looked up at it with wonder in her round blue eyes, the Kangaroo did not jump away, but remained gazing sympathetically at Dot with a slightly puzzled air. Suddenly the big animal seemed to have an idea, and it lightly hopped off into the scrub, where Dot could just see it bobbing up and down as if it were hunting for something. Presently back came the strange Kangaroo with a spray of berries in her funny black hands. They were pretty berries. Some were green, some were red, some blue, and others white. Dot was quite glad to take them when the Kangaroo offered them to her; and as this friendly animal seemed to wish her to eat them, she did so gladly, because she was beginning to feel hungry.

After she had eaten a few berries a very strange thing happened. While Dot had been alone in the bush it had all seemed so dreadfully still. There had been no sound but the gentle stir of a light, fitful breeze in the far-away tree-tops. All around had been so quiet that her loneliness had seemed twenty times more lonely. Now, however, under the influence of these small, sweet berries, Dot was surprised to hear voices everywhere. At first it seemed like hearing sounds in a dream, they were so faint and distant, but soon the talking grew nearer and nearer, louder and clearer, until the whole bush seemed filled with talking.

They were all little voices, some indeed quite tiny whispers and squeaks, but they were very numerous, and seemed to be everywhere. They came from the earth, from the bushes, from the trees, and from the very air. The little girl looked round to see where they came from, but everything looked just the same. Hundreds of ants, of all kinds and sizes, were hurrying to their nests; a few lizards were scuttling about amongst the dry twigs and sparse grasses; there were some grasshoppers, and in the trees birds fluttered to and fro. Then Dot knew that she was hearing, and understanding, everything that was being said by all the insects and creatures in the bush.

All this time the Kangaroo had been speaking, only Dot had been too surprised to listen. But now the gentle, soft voice of the kind animal caught her attention, and she found that the Kangaroo was in the middle of a speech.

"I understood what was the matter with you at once," she was saying, "for I feel just the same myself. I have been miserable, like you, ever since I lost my baby kangaroo. You also must have lost something. Tell me what it is?"

"I've lost my way," said Dot; rather wondering if the Kangaroo would understand her.

"Ah!" said the Kangaroo, quite delighted at her own cleverness, "I knew you had lost something! Isn't it a dreadful feeling? You feel as if you had no inside, don't you? And you're not inclined to eat anything—not even the youngest grass. I have been like that ever since I lost my baby kangaroo. Now tell me," said the creature confidentially, "what your way is like. I may be able to find it for you."

Dot found that she must explain what she meant by saying she had "lost her way", and the Kangaroo was much interested.

"Well," said she, after listening to the little girl, "that is just like you Humans; you are not fit for this country at all! Of course, if you have only one home in one place, you *must* lose it! If you made your home everywhere and anywhere, it would never be lost. Humans are no good in our bush," she continued. "Just look at yourself, now. How do you compare with a Kangaroo? There is your ridiculous sham coat. Well, you have lost bits of it all the way you have come today, and you're nearly left in your bare skin. Now look at my coat. I've done ever so much more hopping than you today, and you see I'm none the worse. I wonder why all your fur grows upon the top of your head," she said reflectively, as she looked curiously at Dot's long flaxen curls. "It's such a silly place to have one's fur the thickest! You see, we have very little there; for we don't want our heads made any hotter under the Australian sun. See how much better off you would be, now that nearly all your sham coat is gone, if that useless fur had been chopped into little, short lengths and spread all over your poor bare body. I wonder why you Humans are made so badly?", she ended, with a puzzled air.

Dot felt for a moment as if she ought to apologize for being so unfit for the bush, and for having all the fur on the top of her head. But, somehow, she had an idea that a little girl must be something better than a kangaroo, although the Kangaroo certainly seemed a very superior person; so she said nothing, but again began to eat the berries.

"You must not eat any more of these berries," said the Kangaroo, anxiously.

"Why?" asked Dot. "They are very nice, and I'm very hungry."

The Kangaroo gently took the spray out of Dot's hand and threw it away. "You see," she said, "if you eat too many of them, you'll know too much."

"One can't know too much," argued the little girl.

"Yes, you can, though," said the Kangaroo, quickly. "If you eat too many of those berries, you'll learn too much, and that gives you indigestion, and then you become miserable. I don't want you to be miserable any more, for I'm going to find your 'lost way'."

The mention of finding her way reminded the little girl of her sad position, which, in her wonder at talking with the Kangaroo, had been quite forgotten for a little while. She became sad again; and seeing how dim the light was getting, her thoughts went back to her parents. She longed to be with them to be kissed and cuddled, and her blue eyes filled with tears.

"Your eyes just now remind me of two fringed violets, with the morning dew on them, or after a shower," said the Kangaroo. "Why are you crying?"

"I was thinking," said Dot.

"Oh, don't think!" pleaded the Kangaroo; "I never do myself."

"I can't help it!" explained the little girl. "What do you do instead?" she asked.

"I always jump to conclusions," said the Kangaroo, and she promptly bounded ten feet at one hop. Lightly springing back again to her position in front of the child, she added, "and that's why I never have a headache."

"Dear Kangaroo," said Dot, "do you know where I can get some water? I'm very thirsty!"

"Of course you are," said her friend; "everyone is at sundown. I'm thirsty myself. But the nearest waterhole is a longish way off, so we had better start at once."

Little Dot got up with an effort. After her long run and fatigue, she was very stiff, and her little legs were so tired and weak, that after a few steps she staggered and fell.

The Kangaroo looked at the child compassionately. "Poor little Human," she said, "your legs aren't much good, and for the life of me, I don't understand how you can expect to get along without a tail. The waterhole is a good way off," she added with a sigh, as she looked down at Dot, lying on the ground, and she was very puzzled what to do. But suddenly she brightened up. "I have an idea," she said joyfully. "Just step into my pouch, and I'll hop you down to the waterhole in less time than it takes a locust to shrill."

Timidly and carefully, Dot did the Kangaroo's bidding, and found herself in the cosiest, softest little bag imaginable. The Kangaroo seemed overjoyed when Dot was comfortably settled in her pouch. "I feel as if I had my dear baby kangaroo again!" she exclaimed; and immediately she bounded away through the tangled scrub, over stones and bushes, over dry watercourses and great fallen trees. And all Dot felt was a gentle rocking motion, and a fresh breeze in her face, which made her so cheerful that she sang this song—

*If you want to go quick,*
*I will tell you a trick*
*For the bush, where there isn't a train.*
*With a hulla-baloo,*
*Hail a big kangaroo—*
*But be sure that your weight she'll sustain.*
*Then with hop, and with skip,*
*She will take you a trip*
*With the speed of the very best steed;*
*And, this is a truth for which I can vouch,*
*There's no carriage can equal a kangaroo's pouch.*
*Oh! where is a friend so strong and true*
*As a dear big, bounding kangaroo?*

*"Good-bye! Good-bye!"*
*The lizards all cry,*
*Each drying its eyes with its tail.*
*"Adieu! Adieu!*
*Dear kangaroo!"*
*The scared little grasshoppers wail.*
*"They're going express*
*To a distant address,"*
*Says the bandicoot, ready to scoot;*
*And your path is well cleared for your progress, I vouch,*
*When you ride through the bush in a kangaroo's pouch.*
*Oh! where is a friend so strong and true*
*As a dear big, bounding kangaroo?*

*"Away and away!"*
*You will certainly say,*
*"To the end of the farthest blue—*
*To the verge of the sky,*
*And the far hills high,*
*O take me with thee, kangaroo!*
*We will seek for the end,*
*Where the broad plains tend,*
*E'en as far as the evening star.*
*Why, the end of the world we can reach, I vouch,*
*Dear kangaroo, with me in your pouch."*
*Oh! where is a friend so strong and true*
*As a dear big, bounding kangaroo?*

# Chapter Two

"THAT is a nice song of yours," said the Kangaroo, "and I like it very much, but please stop singing now, as we are getting near the waterhole, for it's not etiquette to make a noise near water at sundown."

Dot would have asked why everything must be so quiet; but as she peeped out, she saw that the Kangaroo was making a very dangerous descent, and she did not like to trouble her friend with questions just then. They seemed to be going down to a great deep gully that looked almost like a hole in the earth, the depth was so great, and the hills around came so closely together. The way the Kangaroo was hopping was like going down the side of a wall. Huge rocks were tumbled about here and there. Some looked as if they would come rolling down upon them; and others appeared as if a little jolt would send them crashing and tumbling into the darkness below. Where the Kangaroo found room to land on its feet after each bound puzzled Dot, for there seemed no foothold anywhere. It all looked so dangerous to the little girl that she shut her eyes, so as not to see the terrible places they bounded over, or rested on: she felt sure that the Kangaroo must lose her balance, or hop just a little too far or a little too near, and that they would fall together over the side of that terrible wild cliff. At last she said:

"Oh, Kangaroo, shall we get safely to the bottom, do you think?"

"I never think," said the Kangaroo, "but I know we shall. This is the easiest way. If I went through the thick bush on the other side, I should stand a chance of running my head against a tree at every leap, unless I got a stiff neck with holding my head on one side looking out of one eye all the time. My nose gets in the way when I look straight in front," she explained. "Don't be afraid," she continued. "I know every jump of the way. We kangaroos have gone this way ever since Australia began to have kangaroos. Look here!" she said, pausing on a big boulder that hung right over the gully, "we have made a history book for ourselves out of these rocks; and so long as these rocks last, long long after the time when there will be no more kangaroos, and no more humans, the sun, and the moon, and the stars will look down upon what we have traced on these stones."

Dot peered out from her little refuge in the Kangaroo's pouch, and saw the glow of the twilight sky reflected on the top of the boulder. The rough surface of the stone shone with a beautiful polish like a looking-glass, for the rock had been rubbed for thousands of years by the soft feet and tails of millions of kangaroos; kangaroos that had hopped down that way to get water. When Dot saw that, she didn't know why it all seemed solemn, or why she felt such a very little girl. She was a little sad, and the Kangaroo, after a short sigh, continued her way.

As they neared the bottom of the gully the Kangaroo became extremely cautious. She no longer hopped in the open, but made her way with little leaps through the thick scrub. She peeped out carefully before each movement. Her long, soft ears kept moving to catch every sound, and her black sensitive little nose was constantly lifted, sniffing the air. Every now and then she gave little backward starts, as if she were going to retreat by the way she had come, and Dot, with her face pressed against the Kangaroo's soft furry coat, could hear her heart beating so fast that she knew she was very frightened.

They were not alone. Dot could hear whispers from unseen creatures everywhere in the scrub, and from birds in the trees. High up in the branches were numbers of pigeons—sweet little Bronze-Wings; and above all the other sounds she could hear their plaintive voices crying, "We're so frightened! We're so frightened! So thirsty and so frightened! So thirsty and so frightened!"

"Why don't they drink at the waterhole?" whispered Dot.

"Because they're frightened," was the answer.

"Frightened of what?" asked Dot.

"Humans!" said the Kangaroo, in frightened tones and as she spoke she reared up upon her long legs and tail, so that she stood at least six feet high, and peeped over the bushes; her nose working all round, and her ears wagging.

"I think it's safe," she said, as she squatted down again.

"Friend Kangaroo," said a Bronze-Wing that had sidled out to the end of a neighbouring branch, "you are so courageous, will you go first to the water, and let us know if it is all safe? We haven't tasted a drop of water for two days," she said, sadly, "and we're dying of thirst. Last night, when we had waited for hours, to make certain there were no cruel Humans about, we flew down for a drink—and we wanted, oh! so little, just three little sips; but the terrible Humans, with their 'bang-bangs', murdered numbers of us. Then we flew back, and some were hurt and bleeding, and died of their wounds, and none of us have dared to get a drink since." Dot could see that the poor pigeon was suffering from great thirst, for its wings were drooping, and its poor dry beak was open.

The Kangaroo was very distressed at hearing the pigeon's story. "It is dreadful for you pigeons," she said, "because you can only drink at evening; we sometimes can quench our thirst in the day. I wish we could do without water! The Humans know all the waterholes, and sooner or later we all get murdered, or die of thirst. How cruel they are!"

Still the pigeons cried on, "We're so thirsty and so frightened"; and the Bronze-Wing asked the Kangaroo to try again, if she could either smell or hear a Human near the waterhole.

"I think we are safe," said the Kangaroo, having sniffed and listened as before; "I will now try a nearer view."

The news soon spread that the Kangaroo was going to venture near the water, to see if all was safe. The light was very dim, and there was a general whisper that the attempt to get a drink of water should not be left later; as some feared such foes as dingoes and night birds, should they venture into the open space at night. As the Kangaroo moved stealthily forward, pushing aside the branches of the scrub, or standing erect to peep here and there, there was absolute silence in the bush. Even the pigeons ceased to say they were afraid, but hopped silently from bough to bough, following the movements of the Kangaroo with eager little eyes. The Brush Turkey and the Mound-builder left their heaped-up nests and joined the other thirsty creatures, and only by the crackling of the dry scrub, or the falling of a few leaves, could one tell that so many live creatures were together in that wild place.

Presently the Kangaroo had reached the last bushes of the scrub, behind which she crouched.

"There's not a smell or a sound," she said. "Get out, Dot, and wait here until I return, and the Bronze-Wings have had their drink; for, did they see you, they would be too frightened to come down, and would have to wait another night and day."

Dot got out of the pouch, and she was very sorry when she saw how terrified her friend looked. She could see the fur on the Kangaroo's chest moving with the frightened beating of her heart; and her beautiful brown eyes looked wild and strange with fear.

Instantly, the Kangaroo leaped into the open. For a second she paused erect, sniffing and listening, and then she hastened to the water. As she stooped to drink, Dot heard a "whrr, whrr, whrr", and, like falling leaves, down swept the Bronze-Wings. It was a wonderful sight. The waterhole shone in the dim light, with the great black darkness of the trees surrounding it, and from all parts came the thirsty creatures of the bush. The Bronze-Wings were all together. Hundreds of little heads bobbed by the edge of the pool, as the little bills were filled, and the precious water was swallowed; then, together, a minute afterwards, "whrr, whrr, whrr", up they flew, and in one great sweeping circle they regained their tree-tops. Like the bush creatures, Dot also was frightened, and running to the water, hurriedly drank, and fled back to the shelter of the bush, where the Kangaroo was waiting for her.

"Jump in!" said the Kangaroo. "It's never safe by the water," and, a minute after, Dot was again in the cosy pouch, and was hurrying away, like all the others from the water where men are wont to camp, and kill with their guns the poor creatures that come to drink.

That evening the Kangaroo tried to persuade Dot to eat some grass, but as Dot said she had never eaten grass, it got some roots from a friendly Bandicoot, which the little girl ate because she was hungry; but she thought she wouldn't like to be a Bandicoot always to eat such food. Then in a nice dry cave she nestled into the fur of the gentle Kangaroo, and was so tired that she slept immediately.

She only woke up once. She had been dreaming that she was at home, and was playing with the new little calf that had come the day before she was lost, and she couldn't remember, at first waking, what had happened, or where she was. It was dark in the cave, and outside the bushes and trees looked quite black—for there was but little light in that place from the starry sky. It seemed terribly lonesome and wild. When the Kangaroo spoke she remembered everything, and they both sat up and talked a little

"Mo-poke! Mo-poke!" sang the Nightjar in the distance. "I wish the Nightjar wouldn't make that noise when one wants to sleep," said the Kangaroo. "It hasn't got any voice to speak of, and the tune is stupid. It gives me the jim-jams, for it reminds me I've lost my baby kangaroo. There is something wrong about some birds that think themselves musical," she continued; "they are well behaved and considerate enough in the day, but as soon as it is a nice, quiet, calm night, or a bit of a moon is in the sky, they make night hideous to everyone within earshot—'Mo-poke! Mo-poke!' Oh, it gives me the blues!"

As the Kangaroo spoke she hopped to the front of the cave.

"I say, Nightjar," she said, "I'm a little sad tonight. Please go and sing elsewhere.'

"Ah!" said the Nightjar, "I'm so glad I've given you deliciously dismal thoughts with my song! I'm a great artist, and can touch all hearts. That is my mission in the world: when all the bush is quiet, and everyone has time to be miserable, I make them more so—isn't it lovely to be like that?"

"I'd rather you sang something cheerful," said the Kangaroo to herself, but out loud she said, "I find it really too beautiful, it is more than I can bear. Please go a little farther off."

"Mo-poke! Mo-poke!" croaked the Nightjar, farther and farther in the distance, as it flew away.

"What a pity!" said the Kangaroo, as she returned to the cave, "the possum made that unlucky joke of telling the Nightjar it has a touching voice, and can sing; everyone has to suffer for that joke of the possum's. It doesn't matter to him, for he is awake all night, but it is too bad for his neighbours who want to sleep."

Just then there arose from the bush a shrill wailing and shrieking that made Dot's heart stop with fear. It sounded terrible, as if something was wailing in great pain and suffering.

"Oh, Kangaroo!" she cried, "what is the matter?"

"That," said the Kangaroo, as she laid herself down to rest, "is the sound of the Curlew enjoying itself. They are sociable birds, and entertain a great deal. There is a party tonight, I suppose, and that is the expression of their enjoyment. I believe," she continued, with a suppressed yawn, "it's not so painful as it sounds. Willy Wagtail, who goes a great deal amongst Humans, says they do that sort of thing also; he has often heard them when he lived near the town."

Dot had never been in the town, but she was certain she had never heard anything like the Curlew's wailing in her home; and she wondered what Willy Wagtail meant, but she was too sleepy to ask; so she nestled a little closer to the Kangaroo, and with the shrieking of the Curlews, and the mournful note of the distant Mo-poke in her ears, she fell asleep again.

# Chapter Three

WHEN Dot awoke, she did so with a start of fear. Something in her sleep had seemed to tell her that she was in danger. At a first glance she saw that the Kangaroo had left her, and coiled upon her body was a young black Snake. Before Dot could move, she heard a voice from a tree, outside the cave, say, very softly, "Don't be afraid! Keep quite still, and you will not get hurt. Presently I'll kill that Snake. If I tried to do so now it might bite you; so let it sleep on."

She looked up in the direction of the tree, and saw a big Kookaburra perched on a bough, with all the creamy feathers of its breast fluffed out, and its crest very high. The Kookaburra is one of the jolliest birds in the bush, and is always cracking jokes and laughing, but this one was keeping as quiet as he could. Still he could not be quite serious, and a smile played all round his huge beak. Dot could see that he was nearly bursting with suppressed laughter. He kept on saying under his breath, "What a joke this is! What a capital joke! How they'll all laugh when I tell them." Just as if it was the funniest thing in the world to have a Snake coiled up on one's body; when the horrid thing might bite one with its poisonous fangs, at any moment!

Dot said she didn't see any joke, and it was no laughing matter.

"To be sure *you* don't see the joke," said the jovial bird. "Onlookers always see the jokes, and I'm an onlooker. It's not to be expected of you, because you're not an onlooker"; and he shook with suppressed laughter again.

"Where is my dear Kangaroo?" asked Dot.

"She has gone to get you some berries for breakfast," said the Kookaburra, "and she asked me to look after you, and that's why I'm here. That Snake got on you whilst I flew away to consult my doctor, the White Owl, about the terrible indigestion I have. He's very difficult to catch awake; for he's out all night and sleepy all day. He says cockchafers have caused it. The horny wingcases and legs are most indigestible, he assures me. I didn't fancy them much when I ate them last night, so I took his advice and coughed them up, and I'm no longer feeling depressed. Take my advice, and don't eat cockchafers, little Human."

Dot did not really hear all this, nor heed the excellent advice of the Kookaburra, not to eat those hard green beetles that had disagreed with it, for a little shivering movement had gone through the Snake, and presently all the scales of its shining black back and rosy underpart began to move. Dot felt quite sick as she saw the reptile begin to uncoil itself, as it lay upon her. She hardly dared to breathe, but lay as still as if she were dead, so as not to frighten or anger the horrid creature, which presently seemed to slip like a slimy cord over her bare legs, and wriggled away to the entrance of the cave.

With a quick, delighted movement, she sat up, eager to see where the deadly Snake would go. It was very drowsy, having slept heavily on Dot's warm little body; so it went slowly towards the bush, to get some frogs or birds for breakfast. But as it wriggled into the warm morning sunlight outside, Dot saw a sight that made her clap her hands together with anxiety for the life of the jolly Kookaburra.

No sooner did the black Snake get outside the cave, than she saw the Kookaburra fall like a stone from its branch, right on top of the Snake. For a second, Dot thought the bird must have tumbled down dead, it was such a sudden fall; but a moment later she saw it flutter on the ground, in battle with the poisonous reptile, whilst the Snake wriggled and coiled its body into hoops and rings. The Kookaburra's strong wings, beating the air just above the writhing snake, made a great noise, and the serpent hissed in its fierce hatred and anger. Then Dot saw that the Kookaburra's big beak had a firm hold of the Snake by the back of the neck, and that it was trying to fly upwards with its enemy. In vain the dreadful creature tried to bite the gallant bird;

in vain it hissed and stuck out its wicked little spiky tongue; in vain it tried to coil itself round the bird's body; the kookaburra was too strong and too clever to lose its hold, or to let the Snake get power over it.

At last Dot saw that the Snake was getting weaker and weaker for, little by little, the Kookaburra was able to rise higher with it, until it reached the high bough. All the time the Snake was held in the bird's beak, writhing and coiling in agony; for he knew that the Kookaburra had won the battle. But, when the noble bird had reached its perch, it did a strange thing; for it dropped the Snake right down to the ground. Then it flew down again, and brought the reptile back to the bough, and dropped it once more—and this it did many times. Each time the Snake moved less and less, for its back was being broken by these falls. At last the Kookaburra flew up with its victim for the last time, and, holding it on the branch with its foot, beat the serpent's head with its great strong beak. Dot could hear the blows fall—whack, whack, whack—as the beak smote the Snake's head; first on one side, then on the other, until it lay limp and dead across the bough.

"Ah, ah, ah! Ah, ah, ha!" laughed the Kookaburra, and said to Dot, "Did you see all that? Wasn't it a joke? What a capital joke! Ha, ha, ha, ha, ha! Oh, oh, oh! How my sides do ache! What a joke! How they'll laugh when I tell them." Then came a great flight of kookaburras, for they had heard the laughter, and all wanted to know what the joke was. Proudly the Kookaburra told them all about the Snake sleeping on Dot, and the great fight. All the time, first one kookaburra, and then another, chuckled over the story, and when it came to an end every bird dropped its wings, cocked up its tail, and throwing back its head, opened its great beak, and all laughed uproariously together. Dot was nearly deafened by the noise; for some chuckled, some cackled; some said, "Ha, ha, ha!" others said, "Oh, oh, oh!" and as soon as one left off, another began, until it seemed as though they couldn't stop. They all said it was a splendid joke, and that they really must go and tell it to the whole bush. So they flew away, and far and near, for hours, the bush echoed with chuckling and cackling, and wild bursts of laughter, as the kookaburras told that grand joke everywhere.

"Now," said the Kookaburra, when all the others had gone, "a

*The fight between the Kookaburra and the Snake*

bit of snake is just the right thing for breakfast. Will you have some, little Human?"

Dot shuddered at the idea of eating snake for breakfast, and the Kookaburra thought she was afraid of being poisoned.

"It won't hurt you," he said kindly. "I took care that it did not bite itself. Sometimes they do that when they are dying, and then they're not good to eat. But this snake is all right, and won't disagree like cockchafers: the scales are quite soft and digestible," he added.

But Dot said she would rather wait for the berries the Kangaroo was bringing, so the Kookaburra remarked that if she would excuse him, he would like to begin breakfast at once, as the fight had made him hungry.

Then Dot saw him hold the reptile on the branch with his foot, whilst he took its tail into his beak and proceeded to swallow it in a leisurely way. In fact, the Kookaburra was so slow that very little of the snake had disappeared when the Kangaroo returned.

The Kangaroo had brought a pouch full of berries, and in her hand a small spray of the magic ones, by eating which Dot was able to understand the talk of all the bush creatures. All the time she was wandering in the bush the Kangaroo gave her some of these to eat daily, and Dot soon found that the effect of these strange berries only lasted until the next day.

The Kangaroo emptied out her pouch, and Dot found quite a large collection of roots, buds, and berries, which she ate with good appetite.

The Kangaroo watched her eating with a look of quiet satisfaction.

"See," she said, "how easily one can live in the bush without hurting anyone; and yet Humans live by murdering creatures and devouring them. If they are lost in the scrub they die, because they know no other way to live than that cruel one of destroying us all. Humans have become so cruel, that they kill, and kill, not even for food, but for the love of murdering. I often wonder," she said, "why they and the dingoes are allowed to live on this beautiful kind earth. The Black Humans kill and devour us; but they, even, are not so terrible as the Whites, who delight in taking our lives, and torturing us just as an amusement. Every creature in the bush weeps that they should have come to take the beautiful bush away from us."

Dot saw that the sad brown eyes of the Kangaroo were full of tears, and she cried, too, as she thought of all the poor animals and birds that suffer at the hands of white men. "Dear Kangaroo," she said, "if I ever get home, I'll tell everyone of how you unhappy creatures live in fear, and suffer, and ask them not to kill you poor things any more."

But the Kangaroo sadly shook her head, and said: "White Humans are cruel, and love to murder. We must all die. But about your lost way," she continued in a brisk tone, by way of changing this painful subject; "I've been asking about it, and no one has seen it anywhere. Of course, someone must know where it is, but the difficulty is to find the right one to ask." Then she dropped her voice, and came a little nearer to Dot, and stooping down until her little black hands hung close to the ground, she whispered in Dot's ear, "They say I ought to consult the Platypus."

"Could the Platypus help, do you think?" Dot asked.

"I *never* think," said the Kangaroo, "but as the Platypus never goes anywhere, never associates with any other creature, and is hardly ever seen, I conclude it knows everything—it must, you know."

"Of course," said Dot, with some doubt in her tone.

"The only thing is," continued the Kangaroo, once more sitting up and pensively scratching her nose, "the only thing is, I can't bear the Platypus; the sight of it gives me the creeps: it's such a queer creature!"

"I've never seen a Platypus," said Dot. "Do tell me what it is like!"

"I couldn't describe it," said the Kangaroo, with a shudder. "It seems made up of parts of two or three different sorts of creatures. None of us can account for it. It must have been an experiment, when all the rest of us were made; or else it was made up of the odds and ends of the birds and beasts that were left over after we were all finished."

Little Dot clapped her hands. "Oh, dear Kangaroo," she said, "do take me to see the Platypus! There was nothing like that in my Noah's Ark."

"I should say not!" remarked the Kangaroo. "The animals in the Ark said they were each to be of its kind, and every sort of bird and beast refused to admit the Platypus, because it was of so many kinds; and at last Noah turned it out to swim for itself, because there was such a row. That's why the Platypus is so secluded. Ever since then no Platypus is friendly with any other creature, and no animal or bird is more than just polite to it. They couldn't be, you see, because of that trouble in the Ark."

"But that was so long ago," said Dot, filled with compassion for the lonely Platypus; "and, after all, this is not the same Platypus, nor are all the bush creatures the same now as then."

"No," returned the Kangaroo, "and some say there was no Ark, and no fuss over the matter, but that, of course, doesn't make any difference, for it's a very ancient quarrel, so it must be kept up. But if we are to go to the Platypus we had better start now; it is a good time to see it—so come along, little Dot," said the Kangaroo.

# Chapter Four

"GOOD-BYE, Kookaburra!" cried Dot, as they left the cave; and the bird gave her a nod of the head, followed by a wink, which was supposed to mean hearty good-will at parting. He would have spoken, only he had swallowed but part of the Snake, and the rest hung out of the side of his beak, like an old man's pipe; so he couldn't speak. It wouldn't have been polite to do so with his beak full.

Dot was so rested by her sleep all night that she did not ride in the Kangaroo's pouch; but they proceeded together, she walking, and her friend making as small hops as she could, so as not to get too far ahead. This was very difficult for the Kangaroo, because even the smallest hops carried her far in front. After a time they arranged that the friendly animal should hop a few yards, then wait for Dot to catch her up, and then go on again. This she did, nibbling bits of grass as she waited, or playing a little game of hide-and-seek behind the bushes.

Sometimes when she hid like this, Dot would be afraid that she had lost her Kangaroo, and would run here and there, hunting round trees, and clusters of ferns, until she felt quite certain she had lost the kind animal; when suddenly, clean over a big bush, the Kangaroo would bound into view, landing right in front of her. Then Dot would laugh and rush forward and throw her arms around her friend; and the Kangaroo, with a quiet smile, would rub her little head against Dot's curls, and they were both very happy. So, although it was a long and rough way to the little creek where the Platypus lived, it did not seem at all far.

The stream ran at the bottom of a deep gully, that had high rocky sides, with strangely shaped trees growing between the rocks. But, by the stream, Dot thought they must be in fairyland; it was so beautiful. In the dark hollows of the rocks were wonderful ferns; such delicate ones that the little girl was afraid to touch them. They were so tender and green that they could only grow far away from the sun, and as she peeped into the hollows and caves where they grew, it seemed as if she was being shown the secret store-house of Nature, where she kept all the most lovely plants, out of sight of the world. A soft carpet seemed to spring under Dot's feet, like a nice springy mattress, as she trotted along. She asked the Kangaroo why the earth was so soft, and was told that it was not earth, but the dead leaves of the tree-ferns above them, that had been falling for such a long, long time, that no kangaroo could remember the beginning.

Then Dot looked up, and saw that there was no sky to be seen; for they were passing under a forest of tree-ferns, and their lovely spreading fronds made a perfect green tent over their heads. The sunlight that came through was green, as if you were in a house made of green glass. All up the slender stems of these tall tree-ferns were the most beautiful little plants, and many stems were twined, from the earth to their feather-like fronds, with tender creeping ferns—the fronds of which were so fine and close, that it seemed as if the tree-fern were wrapped up in a lovely little fern coat. Even crumbling dead trees, and decaying tree-ferns, did not look dead, because some beautiful moss or lichen, or little ferns had clung to them, and made them more beautiful than when alive.

Dot kept crying out with pleasure at all she saw; especially when little Parakeets, with feathers as green as the ferns, and gorgeous red breasts, came in flocks, and welcomed her to their favourite haunt; and, as she had eaten the berries of understanding, and was the friend of the Kangaroo, they were not frightened, but perched on her shoulders and hands, and chatted their merry talk together. The Kangaroo did not share Dot's enthusiasm for the beauties of the gully. She said it was pretty, certainly, but a bad place for kangaroos, because there was no grass. For her part, she didn't think any sight in nature so lovely as a big plain, green with the little blades of new spring grass. The gully was very showy, but not to her mind so beautiful as the other.

Then they came to a stream that gurgled melodiously as it rippled over stones in its shallow course, or crept round big grey boulders that were wrapped in thick mosses, in which were mingled flowers of the pink and red wild fuchsia, or the creamy great blossoms of the rock-lily. Dot ran down the stream with bare feet, laughing as she paddled in and out among the rocks and ferns, and the sun shone down on the gleaming foam of the water, and made golden lights in Dot's wild curls. The Kangaroo, too, was very merry, and bounded from rock to rock over the stream, showing what wonderful things she could do in that way; and sometimes they paused, side by side, and peeped down upon some still pool that showed their two reflections as in a mirror; and that seemed so funny to Dot that her silvery laugh woke the silence in happy peals, until more green-and-red Parakeets flew out of the bush to join in the fun.

When they had followed the stream some distance, the gully opened out into bush scrub. The little Parakeets then said "Good-bye", and flew back to their favourite tree-ferns and bush growth; and the Kangaroo said that as they were nearing the home of the Platypus, they must not play in the stream any more; to do so might warn the creature of their approach and frighten it. "We shall have to be very careful," she said, "so that the Platypus will neither hear nor smell you. We will therefore walk on the opposite shore as the wind will then blow away from its home."

The stream no longer chattered over rocky beds, but slid between soft banks of earth, under tufts of tall rushes, grasses, and ferns, and soon it opened into a broad pool, which was smooth as glass. The clouds in the sky, the tall surrounding trees, and the graceful ferns and rushes of the banks, were all reflected in the water, so that it looked to Dot like a strange upside-down picture. This, then, was the home of that wonderful animal, and Dot felt quite frightened, because she thought she was going to see something terrible.

At the Kangaroo's bidding, she hid a little way from the edge of the pool, but she was able to see all that happened.

*Dot and the Kangaroo on their way to the Platypus*

The Kangaroo evidently did not enjoy the prospect of conversing with the Platypus. She kept on fidgeting about, putting off calling to the Platypus by one excuse and another: she was decidedly ill at ease.

"Are you frightened of the Platypus?" asked Dot.

"Dear me, no!" replied the Kangaroo, "but I'd rather have a talk with any other bush creature. First of all, the sight of it makes me so uncomfortable that I want to hop away the instant I set eyes upon it. Then, too, it's so difficult to be polite to the Platypus, because one never knows how to behave towards it. If you treat it as an animal, you offend its bird nature, and if you treat it as a bird, the animal in it is mighty indignant. One never knows where one is with a creature that is two creatures," said the Kangaroo.

Dot was so sorry for the perplexity of her friend, that she suggested that they should not consult the Platypus. But the Kangaroo said it must be done, because no one in the bush was so learned. Being such a strange creature, and living in such seclusion, and being so difficult to approach, was a proof that it was the right adviser to seek. So, with a half desperate air, the Kangaroo left the little girl, and went down to the water's edge.

Pausing a moment, she made a strange little noise that was something between a grunt and a hiss: and she repeated this many times. At last Dot saw what looked like a bit of black stick, just above the surface of the pool, coming towards their side. As it moved forward, it left two little silvery ripples that widened out behind it on the smooth waters. Presently the black stick, which was the bill of the Platypus, reached the bank, and the strangest little creature climbed into view. Dot had expected to see something big and hideous; but here was quite a small object after all! It seemed quite ridiculous that the great Kangaroo should be evidently discomposed by the sight.

Dot could not hear what the Kangaroo said, but she saw the Platypus hurriedly prepare to regain the water. It began to stumble clumsily down the bank. The Kangaroo then raised her voice in pleading accents.

"But," she said, "it's such a little Human! I have treated it like my baby kangaroo, and have carried it in my pouch."

This information seemed to arrest the movements of the Platypus;

it had reached the water's edge, but it paused, and turned.

"I tell you," it said in a high-pitched and irritable voice, "that all Humans are alike! They all come here to interview me for the same purpose, and I'm resolved it shall not happen again; I have been insulted enough by their ignorance."

"I assure you," urged the Kangaroo, "that she will not annoy you in that way. She wouldn't think of doing such a thing to any animal."

As the Kangaroo called the Platypus an animal, Dot saw at once that it was offended, and in a great huff it turned towards the pool again. "I beg your pardon," said the Kangaroo nervously. "I didn't mean an altogether animal, or even a bird, but any a—a—a——" She seemed puzzled how to speak of the Platypus, when the strange creature, seeing the well-meaning embarrassment of the Kangaroo, said affably: "Any mammal or Ornithorhynchus Paradoxus."

"Exactly," said the Kangaroo, brightening up, although she hadn't the least idea what a mammal was

"Well, bring the little Human here," said the Platypus in a more friendly tone, "and if I feel quite sure on that point I will permit an interview."

Two bounds brought the Kangaroo to where Dot was hidden. She seemed anxious that the child should make a good impression on the Platypus, and tried with the long claws on her little black hands to comb through Dot's long gleaming curls; but they were so tangled that the child called out at this awkward method of hairdressing, and the Kangaroo stopped. She then licked a black smudge off Dot's forehead, which was all she could do to tidy her. Then she started back a hop, and eyed the child with her head on one side. She was not quite satisfied. "Ah!" she said, "if only you were a baby kangaroo I could make you look so nice! But I can't do anything to your sham coat, which gets worse every day, and your fur is all wrong, for one can't get one's claws through it. You Humans are no good in the bush!"

"Never mind, dear Kangaroo," said the little girl. "When I get home mother will put a new frock on me and will get the tangles out of my hair. Let us go to the Platypus now."

The Kangaroo felt sad as Dot spoke of returning home, for she had become really fond of the little Human. She began to feel that she would be lonely when they parted. However, she did not speak of what was in her mind, but bounded back to the Platypus to wait for Dot.

When the little girl reached the pool, she was still more surprised, on a nearer view of the Platypus, that the Kangaroo should think so much of it. At her feet she beheld a creature like a shapeless bit of wet matted fur. She thought it looked like an empty fur bag that had been fished out of the water. Projecting from the head, that seemed much nearer the ground than the back, was a broad duck's bill, of a dirty grey colour; and peeping out underneath were two fore-feet that were like a duck's also. Altogether it was such a funny object that she was inclined to laugh, only the Kangaroo looked so serious that she tried to look serious, too, as if there was nothing strange in the appearance of the Platypus.

"I am the Ornithorhynchus Paradoxus!" said the Platypus pompously.

"I am Dot," said the little girl.

"Now we know one another's names," said the Platypus, with satisfaction. "If the Kangaroo had introduced us, she would have stumbled over my name and mumbled yours, and we should have been none the wiser. Now tell me, little Human, are you going to write a book about me? Because, if you are, I'm off. I can't stand any more books being written about me; I've been annoyed enough that way."

"I couldn't write a book," said Dot, with surprise; inwardly wondering what anyone could find to make a book of, out of such a small, ugly creature.

"You're quite sure?" asked the Platypus, doubtfully, and evidently more than half inclined to dive into the pool.

"Quite," said Dot.

"Then I'll try to believe you," said the Platypus, clumsily waddling towards some grass, amongst which it settled itself comfortably. "But it's very difficult to believe you Humans, for you tell such dreadful fibs," it continued, as it squirted some dirty water out of a bag that surrounded its bill, and swallowed some water-beetles, small snails and mud that it had stored there. "See, for instance, the way you have all quarrelled and lied about me! One great Human, the biggest fool of all, said I wasn't a live creature at all, but a joke another Human had played upon him. Then they squabbled together —one saying I was a Beaver; another that I was a Duck; another, that I was a Mole, or a Rat. Then they argued whether I was a bird, or an animal, or if we laid eggs or not; and everyone wrote a book, full of lies, all out of his head.

"That's the way Humans amuse themselves. They write books about things they don't understand, and each new book says all the others are all wrong. It's a silly game, and very insulting to the creatures they write about. Humans at the other end of the world, who never took the trouble to come here to see me, wrote books about me. Those who did come were more impudent than those who stayed away. Their idea of learning all about a creature was to dig up its home, and frighten it out of its wits, and kill it; and after a few moons of that sort of foolery they claimed to know all about us. Us! whose ancestors knew the world millions of years before the ignorant Humans came on the earth at all." The Platypus spluttered out more dirty water in its indignation.

The Kangaroo became very timid, as it saw the rising anger of the Platypus, and it whispered to Dot to say something to calm the little creature.

"A million years is a very long time," said Dot; unable at the moment to think of anything better to say. But this remark angered the Platypus more, for it seemed to suspect Dot of doubting what it said.

It clambered up into a more erect position, and its little brown eyes became quite fiery.

"I didn't say a million; I said millions! I can prove by a bone in my body that my ancestors were the Amphitherium, the Amphilestes, the Phascolotherium, and the Stereognathus!" almost shrieked the little creature.

Dot didn't understand what all these words meant, and looked at the Kangaroo for an explanation; but she saw that the Kangaroo didn't understand either, only she was trying to hide her ignorance by a calm appearance, while she nibbled the end of a long grass she held in her fore-paw. But Dot noticed, by the slight trembling of the little black paw, that the Kangaroo was very nervous. She thought she would try and say something to please Platypus; so she asked very kindly if the bone ever hurt it. But this strange creature did not seem to notice the remark. Settling itself more comfortably amongst the grass, it muttered in calmer tones: "I trace my ancestry back to the Oolite Age. Where does man come in?"

"I don't know," said Dot.

"Of course you don't!" replied the Platypus, contemptuously. "Humans are so ignorant! That is because they are so new. When they have existed a few more million years, they will be more like us of old families; they will respect quiet, exclusive living, like that of the Ornithorhynchus Paradoxus, and will not be so inquisitive, pushing, and dangerous as now. The age will come when they will understand, and will cease to write books, and there will be peace for everyone."

The Kangaroo now thought it a good opportunity to change the subject, and gently introduced the topic of Dot's lost way, saying how she had found the little girl, and had taken care of her ever since.

The Platypus did not seem interested, and yawned more than once whilst the Kangaroo spoke.

"The question is," concluded the Kangaroo, "who shall I ask to find it? Someone must know where it is."

"Of course," said the Platypus, yawning again, without so much as putting its web-foot in front of its bill, which Dot thought very rude, or else very ancient manners. "Little Human," it said, "tell me what kind of bush creatures come about your burrow."

"We live in a cottage," she said, but seeing that the Platypus did not like to be corrected, and that the Kangaroo looked quite shocked at her doing so, she hurriedly described the creatures she had seen there. She said there were Crickets, Grasshoppers, Mice, Lizards, Swallows, Opossums, Flying Foxes, Kookaburras, Magpies, and Shepherd's Companions——

"Stop!" interrupted the Platypus, with a wave of its web-foot; "that is the right one."

"Who?" asked the Kangaroo and Dot anxiously together.

"The bird you call Shepherd's Companion. Some of you call it Rickety Dick, or Willy Wagtail." Turning to the Kangaroo especially, it continued: "If you can bring yourself to speak to anything so obtrusive and gossiping, without any ancestry or manners whatever, you will be able to learn all you need from that bird. Humans and Wagtails fraternize together. They're both post-glacial."

"I knew you could advise me," said the Kangaroo, gratefully.

"Oh, Platypus, how clever you are!" cried Dot, clapping her hands.

Directly Dot had spoken she saw that she had offended the queer little creature before her. It raised itself with an air of offended dignity that was unmistakable.

"The name Platypus is insulting," it remarked, looking at the child severely. "It means *broad-footed,* a vulgar pseudonym which could only have emanated from the brutally coarse expressions of a Human. My name is Ornithorhynchus Paradoxus. Besides, even if my front feet can expand, they can also contract; see! as narrow and refined as a bird's claw. Observe, too, that my hind-feet are narrow, and like a seal's fin, though it has been described as a mole's foot."

As the Platypus spoke, and thrust out its strangely different feet, the Kangaroo edged a little closer to Dot and whispered in her ear. "It's getting angry, and is beginning to use long words; do be careful what you say or it will be terrible!"

"I beg your pardon," said Dot; "I did not wish to hurt your feelings, Para—Pa—ra—dox—us."

"*Ornithorhynchus* Paradoxus, if you please," insisted the little creature. "How would you like it if your name was Jones-Smith-Jones, and I called you one Jones, or one Smith, and did not say both the Jones and the Smiths? You have no idea how sensitive our race is. You Humans have no feelings at all compared with ours. Why, my fifth pair of nerves are larger than a man's! Humans get on my nerves dreadfully!" it ended in disgusted accents.

"She did not mean to hurt you," said the gentle Kangaroo, soothingly. "Is there anything we can do to make you feel comfortable again?"

"There is nothing you can do," sighed the Platypus, now mournful and depressed. "I must sing. Only music can quiet my nerves. I will sing a little threnody composed by myself, about the good old days of this world before the Flood." And as it spoke, the Platypus moved into an upright position amongst the tussock grass, and after a little cough opened its bill to sing.

*The Platypus sings of antediluvian days*

The Kangaroo kept very close to Dot, and warned her to be very attentive to the song, and not to interrupt it on any account. Almost before the Kangaroo had ceased to whisper in her ear, Dot heard this strange song, sung to the most peculiar tune she had ever heard, and in the funniest of little squeaky voices.

*The fairest Iguanodon reposed upon the shore;*
*Extended lay her beauteous form, a hundred feet or more.*
*The sun, with rays flammivomous, beat on the blue-black sand;*
*And sportive little Saurians disported on the strand;*
*But oft the Iguanodon reproved them in their glee,*
*And said, "Alas! this Saurian Age is not what it should be!"*

*Then forth from that archaic sea, the Ichthyosaurus*
*Uprose upon his finny wings, with neocomian fuss,*
*"O Iguanodon!" he cried, as he approached the shore,*
*"Why art thou thus dysthynic love? Come, rise with me and soar,*
*Or leave these estuarian seas, and wander in the grove*
*Behold! a bird-like reptile fish is dying for thy love!"*

*Then, through the dark coniferous grove they wandered side by side,*
*The tender Iguanodon and Ichthyosaurian bride;*
*And through the enubilious air, the carboniferous breeze,*
*Awoke, with their amphibious sighs, the silence in the trees.*
*"To think," they cried, botaurus-toned, "when ages intervene,*
*Our osseous fossil forms will be in some museum seen!"*

*Bemoaning thus, by dumous path, they crushed the cycad's growth,*
*And many a crash, and thunder, marked the progress of them both.*
*And when they reached the estuary, the excandescent sun*
*Was setting o'er the hefted sea; their saurian day was done.*
*Then raised they paraseline eyes unto the flaming moon,*
*And wept—the Neocomian Age was passing all too soon!*
*O Iguanodon! O Earth! O Ichthyosaurus!*
*O Melanocephalous saurians! Oh! oh! oh!*

(Here the Platypus was sobbing)

*Oh, Troglyodites obscure—oh! oh!*

At this point of the song, the poor Platypus, whose voice had trembled with increasing emotion and sobbing in each verse, broke down, overcome by the extreme sensitiveness of its fifth pair of nerves and the sadness of its song, and wept in terrible grief.

The gentle Kangaroo was also deeply moved, seeing the Platypus in such sorrow, and Dot mastered her aversion to touching cold, damp fur, and stroked the little creature's head.

The Platypus seemed much soothed by their sympathy, but hurriedly bid them farewell. It said it must try and restore its shattered fifth pair of nerves by a few hydrophilus latipalpus beetles for lunch, and a sleep.

It wearily dragged itself down to the edge of the pool, and looked backwards to the Kangaroo and Dot, who called out "Good-bye" to it. Its eyes were dim with tears, for it was still thinking of the Iguanodon and Ichthyosaurus, and of the good old days before the Flood.

"It breaks my heart to think that they are all fossils," it exclaimed, mournfully shaking its head. "Fossils!" it repeated, as it plunged into the pool and swam away. "Fossils!" it cried once more, in far, faint accents; and a second later it dived out of sight.

For several moments after the Platypus had disappeared from view, the Kangaroo and Dot remained just as it had left them. Then Dot broke the silence.

"Dear Kangaroo," said she, "what was that song about?"

"I don't know," said the animal wistfully, "no one ever knows what the Platypus sings about."

"It was very sad," said Dot.

"Dreadfully sad!" sighed the Kangaroo; "but the Platypus is a most learned and interesting creature," she added hastily. "It's conversation and songs are most edifying; everyone in the bush admits it."

"Does anyone understand its conversation?" asked Dot. She was afraid she must be very stupid, for she hadn't understood anything except that Willy Wagtail could help them to find her way.

"That is the beauty of it all," said the Kangaroo. "The Platypus is so learned and so instructive, that no one tries to understand it; it is not expected that anyone should."

*The prehistoric creatures of the song*

# Chapter Five

"Now we must find Willy Wagtail," said the Kangaroo. "The chances are Click-i-ti-clack, his big cousin who lives in the bush, will be able to tell us where to find him; for he doesn't care for the bush, and lives almost entirely with Humans, and the queer creatures they have brought into the country nowadays. We may have to go a long way, so hop into my pouch, and we will get on our way."

Once more Dot was in the kind Kangaroo's pouch. It was in the latter end of autumn, and the air was so keen that, as her torn little frock was now very little protection to her against the cold, she was glad to be back in that nice fur bag. She was used now to the springy bounding of the great Kangaroo, and felt quite safe; so that she quite enjoyed the wonderful and seemingly dangerous things the animal did in its great leaps and jumps.

With many rests and stops to eat berries or grass on their way, they searched the bush for the rest of the day without finding the big bush Wagtail. All kinds of creatures had seen him, or heard his strange rattling, chattering song, but it always seemed that he had just flown off a few minutes before they heard of him. It was most vexatious, and Dot saw that another night must pass before they would be able to hear of her home. She did not like to think of that, for she could picture to herself all those great men, on their big rough horses, coming back to her father's cottage that night, and how they would begin to be quiet and sad.

She thought it would not be half so bad to be lost, if the people at home could only know that one was safe and snug in a kind Kangaroo's pouch; but she knew that her parents could never suppose that she was so well cared for, and would only think that she was dying alone in the terrible bush—dying for want of food and water, and from fear and exposure. How strange it seemed that people should die like that in the bush, where so many creatures lived well, and happily! But then they had no bush friends to tell them what berries and roots to eat, and where to get water, and to cuddle them up in a nice warm fur during the cold night. As she thought of this she rubbed her face against the Kangaroo's soft coat, and patted her with her little hands; and the affectionate animal was so pleased at these caresses, that she jumped clean over a watercourse, twenty feet at least, in one bound.

It was getting evening time, and the sun was setting with a beautiful rosy colour, as they came upon a lovely scene. They had followed the watercourse until it widened out into a great shallow creek beside a grassy plain. As they emerged from the last scattered bushes and trees of the forest, and hopped out into the open side of a range of hills, miles and miles of grass country, with dim distant hills, stretched before them. The great shining surface of the creek caught the rosy evening light, and every pink cloudlet in the sky looked doubly beautiful reflected in the water. Here and there out of the water arose giant skeleton trees, with huge silver trunks and contorted dead branches. On these twisted limbs were numbers of birds: Shag, blue and white Cranes, and black and white Ibis with their bent bills. Slowly paddling on the creek, with graceful movements, were twenty or thirty black Swans, and in and out of their ranks, as they passed in stately procession, shot wild Ducks and Moor Hens, like a flotilla of little boats amongst a fleet of big ships. All these birds were watching a pretty sight that arrested Dot's attention at once. By the margin of the creek, where tufted rushes and tall sedges shed their graceful reflection on the pink waters, were a party of Native Companions dancing.

"In these times it is seldom we can see a sight like this," said the Kangaroo. "The water is generally too unsafe for the birds to enjoy themselves. It often means death to them to have a little pleasure."

As the Kangaroo spoke, one of the Native Companions caught sight of her, and leaving the dance, opened her wings, and still making dainty steps with her long legs, half-danced and half-flew to where the Kangaroo was sitting.

"Good evening, Kangaroo," she said, gracefully bowing. "Will you not come a little nearer to see the dance?" Then the Native Companion saw Dot in the Kangaroo's pouch, and made a little spring of surprise. "Dear me!" she said, "what have you in your pouch?"

"It's a Human," said the Kangaroo apologetically; "it's quite a little harmless one. Let me introduce you."

So Dot alighted from the pouch, and joined in the conversation, and the Native Companion was much interested in hearing her story.

"Do you dance?" asked the Native Companion, with a quick turn of her head, on its long, graceful neck. Dot said that she loved dancing. So the Native Companion took her down to the creek, and all the other Companions stopped dancing and gathered round her, whilst she was introduced and her story told. Then they spread their wings, and with stately steps escorted her to the edge of the water, whilst the Kangaroo sat a little way off, and delightedly watched the proceedings.

Dot didn't understand any of the figures of the dance; but the scenery was so lovely, and so was the pink sunset, and the Native Companions were so elegant and gay, that, catching up her ragged little skirts in both hands, she followed their movements with her bare brown feet as best she could, and enjoyed herself very much. To Dot, the eight birds that took part in the entertainment were very tall and splendid, with their lovely grey plumage and greeny heads, and she felt quite small as they gathered round her sometimes, and enclosed her within their outspread wings. And how beautiful their dancing was! How light their dainty steps as their feet scarcely touched the earth! And what fantastic measures they danced—advancing, retreating, circling round—with their beautiful wings keeping the rhythm of their feet. There was one figure that Dot thought the prettiest of all—when they danced in line at the margin of the water; stepping, and bowing, and gracefully gyrating to their shadows, which were reflected with the pink clouds of evening on the surface of the creek.

*Dot dances with the Native Companions*

Dot was very sorry, and hot, and breathless, when the dance came to an end. The sun had been gone a long time, and all the pink shades had slowly turned to grey; the creek had lost its radiant colour, and looked like a silver mirror, and so desolate and sombre that no one could have imagined it to have been the scene of so much gaiety shortly before.

Dot hastily returned to the Kangaroo, and all the Native Companions came daintily and made graceful adieus to them both. Afterwards, they spread their great, soft wings, and, stretching their long legs behind them, wheeled upwards to the darkening sky. Then all the birds in the bare trees preened their feathers, and settled down for the night; and the Kangaroo took her little Human charge back to the bush, where there was a cosy sheltering rock, under which to pass the night, and they lay down together, with the stars peeping at them through the branches of the trees.

They had slept for a long time, as it seemed to Dot, when they were awakened by a little voice saying:

"Wake up, Kangaroo! You are in danger. Get away as soon as possible!"

The moon was shining fitfully as it broke through swift-flying clouds. In the uncertain light, Dot could see a little creature near them, and knew at once that it was an Opossum.

"What is the matter?" asked the Kangaroo, softly. "Blacks!" said the Opossum. And as it spoke, Dot heard a sound as of a half-dingo dog howling and snapping in the distance. As that sound was heard, the Opossum made one flying leap to the nearest tree and scrambled out of sight in a moment

"I wish he had told us a little more," said the Kangaroo. "Still, for a possum, it was a good-natured act to wake me up. They are selfish, spiteful little beasts, as a rule. Now I wonder where those blacks are? I shall have to go a little way to sniff and listen. I won't go far, so don't be afraid, but stay quietly here until I come back."

# Chapter Six

It was terrible to Dot to see the Kangaroo hop off into the dark bush, and to find herself all alone; so she crawled out from under the ledge of rock into the moonlight, and sat on a stone where she could see the sky, and watch the black ragged clouds hurry over the moon. But the bush was not altogether quiet. She could hear an owl hooting at the moon. Not far off was a camp of quarrelsome Flying Foxes, and the melancholy Nightjar in the distance was fulfilling its mission of making all the bush creatures miserable with its incessant, mournful "Mo-poke! Mo-poke!" As Dot could understand all the voices, it amused her to listen to the wrangles of the Flying Foxes, as they ate the fruit of a wild fig-tree near by. She saw them swoop past on their huge black wings with a solemn flapping. Then, as each little Fox approached the tree, the Foxes who were there already screamed, and swore in dreadfully bad language at the visitor. For every little Fox on the tree was afraid some other Flying Fox would eat all the figs, and as each visitor arrived he was assailed with cries of, "Get away! You're not wanted here!"

"This is my branch; my figs!"

"Go and find figs for yourself!"

"These figs are not half-ripe like the juicy ones on the other side of the tree!"

Then the newcomer Flying Fox, with a spiteful squeal, would pounce down on a branch already occupied, and angry spluttering and screams would arise, followed by a heavy fall of fighting Foxes tumbling with a crash through the trees. Then out into the open sky swept dozens of black wings, accompanied by abusive swearing from dozens of wicked little brown Foxes; and, as they settled again on the tree, all the fighting would begin again, so that the squealing, screaming, and swearing never ended.

As Dot was listening to the fighting of the Flying Foxes, she heard a sound near her that alarmed her greatly. It was impossible to say what the noise was like. It might have been the braying of a donkey mixed with the clattering of palings tumbled together, and with grunts and snorts. Dot started to her feet in fright, and would have run away, only she was afraid of being lost worse than ever, so she stood still and looked round for the terrible monster that could make such extraordinary sounds. The grunts and clattering stopped, and the noise died away in a long doleful bray, but she could not see where it came from. Having peered into the dark shadows, Dot went more into the open, and sat with her back to a fallen tree, keeping an anxious watch all round.

"Perhaps it is the blacks. What would they do with me if they found me? What will happen if they have killed my dear Kangaroo?" And she covered her face with her hands as this terrible thought came into her head. Soon she heard something coming towards her stealthily and slowly. She would not look up, she was so frightened. She was sure it was some fierce-looking black man, with his spear, about to kill her. She shut her eyes closer, and held her breath. "Perhaps," she thought, "he will not see me." Then a cold shiver went through her little body as she felt something claw hold of her hair, and she thought she was about to be killed. She kept her eyes shut, and the clawing went on, and then to her astonishment she heard an animal voice say in wondering tones:

"Why, it's fur! How funny it looked in the moonlight!"

Then Dot opened her eyes very wide and looked round, and saw a funny Native Bear on the tree-trunk behind her. He was quite clearly to be seen in the moonlight. His thick, grey fur, that looked as if he was wrapped up to keep out the most terrible cold weather; his short, stumpy, big legs, and little sharp face with big bushy ears, could be seen as distinctly as in daylight. Dot had never seen one so near before, and she loved it at once. It looked so innocent and kind.

"You dear little Native Bear!" she exclaimed, at once stroking its head.

"Am I a Native Bear?" asked the animal in a meek voice. "I never heard that before. I thought I was a Koala. I've always been told so, but of course one never knows oneself. What are you? Do you know?"

"I'm a little girl," replied Dot, proudly.

The Koala saw that Dot was proud, but as it didn't see any reason why she should be, it was not a bit afraid of her.

"I never heard of one or saw one before," it said, simply. "Do you burrow, or live in a tree?"

"I live at home," said Dot; but, wishing to be quite correct, she added: "that is, when I am there."

"Then, where are you now?" asked the Koala, rather perplexed.

"I'm not at home," replied Dot, not knowing how to make her position clear to the little animal.

"Then you live where you don't live?" said the Koala. "Where is it?" and the little bear looked quite unhappy in its attempt to understand what Dot meant.

"I've lost it," said Dot. "I don't know where it is."

"You make my head feel empty," said the Koala, sadly. "I live in the gum-tree over there. Do you eat gum-leaves?"

"No. When I'm at home I have milk, and bread, and eggs, and meat."

"Dear me!" said the Koala. "They're all new to me. Is it far? I should like to see the trees they grow on. Please show me the way."

"But I can't," said Dot; "they don't grow on trees, and I don't know my way home. It's lost, you see."

"I don't see," said the Native Bear. "I never can see far at night, and not at all in daylight. That is why I came here. I saw your fur shining in the moonlight, and I couldn't make out what it was, so I came to see. If there is anything new to be seen, I must get a near view of it. I don't feel happy if I don't know all about it. Aren't you cold?"

"Yes, I am, a little, since my Kangaroo left me," Dot said.

"Now you make my head feel empty again," said the Koala, plaintively. "What has a Kangaroo got to do with your feeling cold? What have you done with your fur?"

*Dot, the Native Bear, and the Opossum*

"I never had any," said Dot, "only these curls," and she touched her little head.

"Then you ought to be black," argued the Koala. "You're not the right colour. Only blacks have no fur, but what they steal from the proper owners. Do you steal fur?" it asked in an anxious voice.

"How do they steal fur?" asked Dot.

The Koala looked very miserable and spoke with horror: "They kill us with spears and tear off our skins and wear them because their own skins are no good."

"That's not stealing," said Dot; "that's killing." And, although it seemed very difficult to make the little bear understand, she explained: "Stealing is taking away another person's things; and when a person is dead he hasn't anything belonging to him, so it's not stealing to take what belonged to him before, because it isn't his any longer—that is, if it doesn't belong to anyone else."

"You make my head feel empty," complained the Koala. "I'm sure you're all wrong; for an animal's skin and fur is his own, and it's his life's business to keep it whole. Everyone in the bush is trying to keep his skin whole, all day long, and all night, too. Good gracious! What is the matter up there?"

A terrible hullabaloo between a pair of Opossums up a neighbouring gum-tree arrested the attention of both Dot and the Koala. Presently the sounds of snarling, spitting, and screaming ended, and an Opossum climbed out to the far end of a branch, where the moonlight shone on his grey fur like silver. There he remained snapping and barking disagreeable things to his mate, who climbed up to the topmost branch, and snarled and growled back equally unpleasant remarks.

"Why don't you bring in gum-leaves for tomorrow, instead of sleeping all day and half the night, too?" shouted the Opossum on the branch to his wife. "You know I get hungry before daylight is over and hate going out in the light."

"Get them yourself, you lazy loon!" retorted the lady Opossum. "If you disturb my dreams again this way, I'll make your fur fly."

"Take care!" barked back her husband, "or I'll bring you off that branch pretty quickly."

"You'd better try!" sneered his wife. "Remember how I landed you into the billabong the other night!"

The taunt was too much for the Opossum on the branch. He scuttled up the tree to reach his mate, who sprang forward from her perch into the air. Dot saw her spring with her legs all spread out, so that the skinny flaps were like furry wings. By this means she was able to break her fall, and softly alighting on the earth, a moment after, she had scrambled up another tree, followed by her mate. From tree to tree, from branch to branch, they fled or pursued one another, with growls, screams, and splutters, until they disappeared from sight.

"How unhappy those poor Opossums must be, living in the same tree," said Dot. "Why don't they live in different trees?"

"They wouldn't be happy," observed the Koala, "they are so fond of one another."

"Then why do they quarrel?" asked Dot.

"Because they live in the same tree, of course," said the Koala. "If they lived in different trees, and never quarrelled, they wouldn't like it at all. They'd find life dull, and they'd get sulky. There's nothing worse than a sulky possum. They are champions at that."

"They made a dreadful noise with their quarrelling," said Dot. "They are nearly as bad as the Flying Foxes over there. I wonder if they made that fearful sound I heard just before you came?"

"I expect what you heard was from me," said the Koala. "I had just awakened, and when I saw the moon was up I felt pleased."

"Was all that sound and many noises yours?" asked Dot in astonishment, as she regarded the shaggy little animal on the tree-trunk.

The Koala smiled modestly. "Yes!" it said; "when I'm pleased there is no creature in the bush can make such a noise, or so many different noises at once. I waken everyone for a quarter of a mile round. You wouldn't think it, to see me as I am, would you?" The Koala was evidently very pleased with this accomplishment.

"It isn't kind of you to wake up all the sleeping creatures," said Dot.

"Why not?" asked the Koala. "You are a night creature, I suppose, or you wouldn't be awake now. Well, don't you think it unfair the way everything is arranged for the day creatures?"

"But, then," said Dot, "there are so many more day creatures."

"That doesn't make any difference," observed the Koala.

"But it does," said Dot.

"How?" asked the Native Bear.

"Because if you had the day it wouldn't be any good to you, and if they had the night it wouldn't be any good to them. So your night couldn't be their day, and their day couldn't be your night."

"You make my head feel empty," said the Koala. "But you'd think differently if a flock of Kookaburras settled on your tree, and guffawed idiotically when you wanted to sleep."

"As you don't like being waked yourself, why do you wake others then?" asked Dot.

"Because this is a free country," said the Koala.

While Dot was trying to understand why the Koala's reason should suffice for one animal making another's life uncomfortable, she rejoiced to see the Kangaroo bound into sight. She forgot all about the Koala, and rushed forward to meet it.

# Chapter Seven

"I'M so glad you've come back!" she exclaimed.

The Kangaroo was a little breathless and excited. "We are not in danger at present," she said, "but one never knows when one will be, so we must move; and that will be more dangerous than staying where we are."

"Then let us stay," said Dot.

"That won't do," replied the Kangaroo. "This is the conclusion I have jumped to. If we stay here, the blacks might come this way and their dingo dogs hunt us to death. To get to a safe place we must pass their camp. That is a little risky, but we must go that way. We can do this easily if the dogs don't get scent of us, as all the blacks are prancing about and making a noise, having a kind of game, in fact, and they are so amused that we ought to get past quite safely. I've done it many times before at night."

Dot looked round to say good-bye to the Koala, but the little animal had heard the Kangaroo speak of blacks, and that word suggested to its empty little head that it must keep its skin whole, so, without waiting to be polite to Dot, it had sneaked up its gum-tree and was well out of sight.

Without wasting time, Dot settled in the Kangaroo's pouch, and they started upon their perilous way.

For some distance the Kangaroo hopped along boldly, with an occasional warning to Dot to shut her eyes as they plunged through the bushes; but after crossing a watercourse, and climbing a stiff hill, she whispered that they must both keep quite silent, and told Dot to listen as she stopped for a moment.

Dot could hear to their right a murmuring of voices and a steady beating sound.

"Their camp is over there," said the Kangaroo. "That is the sound of their game."

"Can't we go some other way?" asked Dot.

"No," answered the Kangaroo, "because past that place we can reach some very wild country where it would be hard for them to pursue us. We shall have to pass quite close to their playground." So in perfect silence they went on.

The Kangaroo seemed to Dot to approach the whereabouts of the blackfellows as cautiously as when they had visited the waterhole the first night. Dot's little heart beat fast as the sound of the blacks' corroboree became clearer and clearer and they neared the scene of the dance. Soon she could hear the stamping of feet, the beating of weapons together, and the wild chanting; and sometimes there were the whimpering of dogs, and the cry of children at the camp and a little distance from the corroboree ground.

The Kangaroo showed no signs of fear at the increasing noise of the blacks, but every sound of a dog caused it to stop and twist about its big ears and sensitive nose, as it sniffed and listened.

Soon Dot could see a great red glare of firelight through the trees ahead of their track, and she knew that in that place the tribe of black men were having a festive dance.

If they had gone on their way it is possible that they would have slipped past the blacks without danger. But although the Kangaroo is as timid an animal as any in the bush, it is also very curious, and Dot's Kangaroo wished to peep at the corroboree. She whispered to Dot that it would be nice for a little Human to see some other Humans after being so long amongst bush creatures, and said, also, that there would be no great danger in hopping to a rock that would command a view of the open ground where the corroboree was being held. Of course, Dot thought this would be great fun, so the Kangaroo took her to the rock, where they peeped through the trees and saw before them the weird scene and dance.

*The Corroboree*

Dot nearly screamed with fright at the sight. She had thought she would see a few black folk, not a crowd of such terrible people as she beheld. They did not look like human beings at all, but like dreadful demons; they were so wicked and ugly in appearance. The men who were dancing were without clothes, but their black bodies were painted with red and white stripes, and bits of down and feathers were stuck on their skin. Some had only white stripes over the places where their bones were, which made them look like skeletons flitting before the fire, or in and out of the surrounding darkness. The dancing men were divided from the rest of the tribe by a row of fires, which, burning brightly, lit the horrid scene with a lurid red light. The firelight seemed to make the ferocious faces of the tribe still more hideous.

The tribe people were squatting in rows on the ground, beating boomerangs and spears together, or striking bags of skin with sticks, to make an accompaniment to the wailing song they sang. Sometimes the women would cease beating the skin bags to clap their hands and strike their sides, yelling the words of the corroboree song, as the painted figures, like fiends and skeletons, danced before the row of fires.

It was a terrifying sight to Dot. "Oh, Kangaroo!" she whispered, "they are dreadful, horrid creatures."

"They're just Humans," replied the Kangaroo indulgently.

"But white Humans are not like that," said Dot.

"All Humans are the same underneath; they all kill kangaroos," said the Kangaroo. "Look there! They are playing at killing us in their dance."

Dot looked once more at the hideous figures as they left the fire and began acting like actors. One of the blackfellows had come from a little bower of trees, and wore a few skins so arranged as to make him look as much like a kangaroo as possible, whilst he worked a stick which he pretended was a kangaroo's tail, and hopped about. The other painted savages were creeping in and out of the bushes with their spears and boomerangs as if they were hunting, and the dressed-up kangaroo made believe not to see them, but stooped down, nibbling grass.

"What an idea of a kangaroo!" sniffed Dot's friend. "Why, a real kangaroo would have smelt or heard those Humans, and have bounded away far out of sight by now."

"But it's all sham," said Dot. "The black man couldn't be a real kangaroo."

"Then it just shows how stupid Humans are to try to be one," said her friend. "Humans think themselves so clever," she continued, "but just see what bad kangaroos they make—such a simple thing to do, too! But their legs bend the wrong way for jumping, and that stick isn't any good for a tail, and it has to be worked with those big, clumsy arms. Just see, too, how those skins fit! Why, it's enough to make a kangaroo's sides split with laughter to see such foolery!" Dot's friend peeped at the black's acting with the contempt to be expected of a real kangaroo, who saw human beings pretending to be one of those noble animals. Dot thought the Kangaroo had never looked so grand before. She was so tall, so big, and yet so graceful: a really beautiful creature.

"Well, that's over!" remarked the Kangaroo, as one of the blacks pretended to spear the dressed-up blackfellow, and all the rest began to dance around, whilst the sham kangaroo made believe to be dead. "Well, I forgive their killing such a silly creature! There wasn't a jump in it."

After more dancing to the singing and noise of the onlookers, a blackfellow came from the little bower in the dim background, with a battered straw hat on, and a few rags tied round his neck and wrists, in imitation of a collar and cuffs. The fellow tried to act the part of a white man, although he had no more clothes on than the old hat and rags. But, after a great deal of dancing, he strutted about, pulled up the rag collar, made a great fuss with his rag cuffs, and kept taking off his old straw hat to the other blackfellows, and to the rest of the tribe, who kept up the noise on the other side of the fires.

"Now this is better!" said the Kangaroo, with a smile. "It's very silly, but Willy Wagtail says that is just the way Humans go on in the town. Black Humans can play at being white Humans, but they are no good as kangaroos."

Dot thought that if men behave like that in towns it must be very strange. She had not seen any like the acting blackfellow at her cottage home. But she did not say anything, for it was quite clear in her little mind that blackfellows, kangaroos, and willy wagtails had a very poor opinion of white people. She felt that they must all be wrong; but, all the same, she sometimes wished she could be a noble kangaroo, and not a despised human being

"I wish I were not a little white girl," she whispered to the Kangaroo.

The gentle animal patted her kindly with her delicate black hands.

"You are as nice now as my baby kangaroo," she said sadly, "but you will have to grow into a real white Human. For some reason there have to be all sorts of creatures on the earth. There are hawks, snakes, dingoes and humans, and no one can tell for what good they exist. They must have dropped on to this world by mistake for another, where there could only have been themselves. After all," said the kind animal, "it wouldn't do for everyone to be a kangaroo, for I doubt if there would be enough grass; but you may become an improved Human."

"How could I be that?" asked Dot, eagerly.

"Never wear kangaroo leather boots—never use kangaroo skin rugs, and"—here it hesitated a little, as though the subject were a most unpleasant one to mention.

"Never do what?" inquired Dot, anxious to know all that she should do, so as to be improved.

"Never, never eat kangaroo-tail soup!" said the Kangaroo, solemnly.

"I never will," said Dot, earnestly, "I will be an improved Human."

This conversation had been so serious to both Dot and the Kangaroo, that they had quite forgotten the perilousness of their position. Perhaps this was because the kangaroo cannot think, but it quickly jumped to the conclusion that they were in danger.

Whilst they had been peeping at the corroboree, and talking, the dingo dogs that had been prowling around the camp, had caught scent of the Kangaroo; and, following the trail, had set up an angry snapping and howling.

The instant this sound was heard by the Kangaroo, she made an immense bound, and as she seemed to fly through the bush, Dot could hear the sounds of the corroboree give place to a noise of shouting and disorder: the dingo dogs and the blacks were all in pursuit, and Dot's Kangaroo, with little Dot in her pouch, was leaping and bounding at a terrific pace to save both their lives!

# Chapter Eight

It was fortunate that the Kangaroo could not think of all that might befall them, or she would never have had the courage for the wonderful feats of jumping she performed. Poor little Dot, whose busy brain pictured all kinds of terrible fates, was so overcome with fear that she seemed hardly to know what had happened; and the more she thought, the more terrified she became.

The Kangaroo did not attempt to continue the upward ascent, but followed a slope of the rugged hill, leaping from rock to rock. This was better than trying to escape where the trees and scrubs would have prevented her making those astonishing bounds. But the clouds had left the moon clear for a while, so that the blackfellows and the dogs easily followed every movement, as they pursued the hunt on a smoother level below. The blacks were trying to hurry on, so as to cut off the Kangaroo's retreat at a spur of the hill, where, to get away, she would have to leave the rocks and descend towards them. In the meantime Dot's ears were filled with the sounds of snarling snaps from the dingo dogs, and hideous noises from the blacks, encouraging the animals to attack the Kangaroo. But what pained her most were the gasps and little moans of her good friend, as she put such tremendous power into every leap she made for their lives; crashing through twigs and scattering stones and pebbles in the wild speed of their flight.

Then Dot's busy little brain told her another thing, which made her more miserable. It was becoming quite clear that the poor Kangaroo was getting rapidly exhausted, owing to her having to bear

Dot's weight. Her panting became more and more distressing, and so did her sad moans; and flecks of foam from her straining lips fell on Dot's face and hands. Dot knew that her Kangaroo was trying to save her at the risk of her own life. Without the little girl in her pouch, she might get away safely; but, with her to carry, they would both probably fall victims to the fierce blacks and their dogs.

"Kangaroo! Kangaroo!" she cried, "put me down! Drop Dot anywhere, anywhere, but don't get killed yourself!"

But all Dot heard was a little hissing sound from the brave animal, which sounded like, "Never again!"

"You will be killed," moaned Dot.

"Together!" said the little hissing voice, as another great bound brought them to the spur of the hill; and then the Kangaroo had to pause.

In that moment Dot seemed to hear and see everything. They were perched on a rock, and the moonlight lit all their surroundings like day. To the right was a deep black chasm, with a white foaming waterfall pouring into the darkness below. In front was the same wide chasm, only less wide, and beyond it, on the other side of the great yawning cleft in the earth, was a wild spread of morass country—a gloomy, terrible-looking place. To the left was a steep slope of small rocks and stones, leading downwards to the hollow of sedgy land that fringed the cliffs to the chasm. The only retreat possible was to pass down this declivity, and try to escape by the sedgy land, and this is what the black huntsmen had expected. It was a very weird and desolate place; and everything looked dark and dismal, under the moonlight, as it streamed between stormy black clouds. In that light Dot could see the blacks hurrying forward. Already one of the dogs had far out-run the others, and with wolfish gait and savage sounds, was pressing towards their place of observation.

The panting, trembling Kangaroo saw the approaching dog, also, and leaped down from the crag. As she dropped to earth, she stooped, and quickly lifted Dot out of her pouch, and, almost before Dot could realize the movement, she found herself standing alone, whilst the Kangaroo hopped forward to the front of a big boulder, as if to meet the dog. Here the poor hunted creature took her stand, with her back close to the rock. Gentle and timid as she was, and unfitted by nature to fight for her life against fierce odds, it was brave indeed of the poor Kangaroo to face her enemies, prepared to do battle for the lives of little Dot and herself.

So noble did Dot's Kangaroo look in that desperate moment, standing erect, waiting for her foe, and conquering her naturally frightened nature by a grand effort of courage, that it seemed impossible that either dogs or men should be so cruel as to take her life. For a moment the dingo hound seemed daunted by her bravery, and paused a little way off, panting, with its great tongue lolling out of its mouth. Dot could see its sharp wicked teeth gleaming in the moonlight. For a few seconds it hesitated to make the attack, and looked back down the slope, to see if the other dogs were coming to help; but they were only just beginning the ascent, and the shouting blackfellows were farther off still. Then the dog could no longer control its savage nature. It longed to leap at the poor Kangaroo's throat—that pretty furry throat that Dot's arms had so often encircled lovingly, and it was impatient to fix its terrible teeth there, and hold, and hold, in a wild struggle, until the poor Kangaroo should gradually weaken from fear and exhaustion, and be choked to death. These thoughts filled the dog with a wicked joy. It wouldn't wait any longer for the other dingo hounds. It wanted to murder the Kangaroo all by itself; so, with a toss of its head, and a terrible snarl, it sprang forward ferociously, with open jaws, aiming at the victim's throat.

Dot clasped her cold hands together. Tears streamed down her cheeks, and her little voice, choking with sobs, could only wail, "Oh, dear Kangaroo! My dear Kangaroo! Don't kill my dear Kangaroo!" and she ran forward to throw herself upon the dog and try to save her friend.

But before the terrified little girl could reach the big rock, the dog had made its spring upon her friend. The brave Kangaroo, instead of trying to avoid her fierce enemy, opened her little arms, and stood erect and tall to receive the attack. The dog, in its eagerness, and owing to the nature of the ground, misjudged the distance it had to spring. It failed to reach the throat it had aimed at, and in a moment the Kangaroo had seized the hound in a tight embrace. There was a momentary struggle, the dog snapping and trying to free itself, and the Kangaroo holding it firmly. Then she used the only

*A leap for life*

weapon she had to defend herself from dogs and men—the long sharp claw in her foot. Whilst she held the dog in her arms, she raised her powerful leg, and with that long, strong claw, tore open the dog's body. The dog yelped in pain as the Kangaroo threw it to the ground, where it lay rolling in agony and dying; for the Kangaroo had given it a terrible wound. The other dogs were still some distance below, and the cries of their companion caused them to pause in fear and wonder, while the black men could be seen advancing in the dim light, flourishing their spears and boomerangs.

It was quite impossible to retreat that way; and where Dot and her Kangaroo were, they were hemmed in by a rocky cliff and the deep black chasm. The Kangaroo saw at a glance where lay their only chance of life. She picked up Dot, placed her in her pouch, and without a word leaped forward towards that fearful gulf of darkness and foaming waters. As they neared the spot, Dot saw that the hunted animal was going to try and leap across to the other side. It seemed impossible that with one bound she could span that terrible place and reach the sedged morass beyond; and still more impossible that it should be done by the poor animal with heavy Dot in her pouch. Again Dot cried, "Oh, darling Kangaroo, leave me here, and save yourself. You can never, never do it carrying me!"

All she heard was something like "try" or "we'll die". She could not make out what the Kangaroo said, for the crashing of the waterfall, the whistling of the wind, and the scattering of stones as they dashed forward, made such a storm of noises in her ears. She could see when they reached the grassy fringe of the precipice, where the Kangaroo was able to quicken her pace, and literally seemed to fly to their fate. Then came the last bound before the great spring. Dot held her breath, and a feeling of sickness came over her. Her head seemed giddy, and she could not see, but she clasped her hands together and said, "God help my Kangaroo!" and then she felt the fearful leap and rush through the air.

Yes! They had just reached the other side. No, they had not quite: what was the matter? What a struggle! Stones falling, twigs and grasses wrenching, the courageous Kangaroo fighting for a foothold on the very brink of the precipice. What a terrible moment! Every second Dot felt sure they would fall backward and drop deep into the gully below, to be dashed to pieces on the rocks and tree-tops. But God did help Dot's Kangaroo; the little reeds and rushes held tightly in the earth, and the poor struggling animal, exerting all her remaining strength, gained the reedy slope safely. She staggered forward for a few reeling hops, and then fell to the earth like a dead creature. In an instant Dot was out of the pouch and had her arm round the poor animal's neck, crying, as she saw blood and foam oozing from her mouth, and a strange dim look in her sad eyes.

"Don't die, dear Kangaroo! Oh, please don't die!" cried Dot, wringing her hands, and burying her face in the fur of the poor gasping creature.

"Dot," panted the Kangaroo, "make a noise! Cry aloud! Not safe yet!"

The little girl didn't understand why the Kangaroo wanted her to make a noise, and she had, in her fear and sorrow, quite forgotten their pursuers. But now she turned, and could hear the blacks urging on their dogs as they were making an attempt to skirt round the precipice and gain the other side of the chasm. So Dot did as she was told, and screamed and cried like the most naughty of children; and the gasping Kangaroo told her to go on doing so.

Then what seemed to Dot a very terrifying thing happened; for she soon heard other cries mingle with hers. From the desolate morass, and from the gully in darkness below, came the sound of a bellowing. She stopped crying and listened, and could hear those awesome voices all round, and the echoes made them still more hobgoblinish. The Kangaroo's eyes brightened, as she restrained her panting, and listened also. "Go on," she said, "we're safe now," so Dot made more crying, and her noises and the others would have frightened anyone who had heard them in that lonely place, with the wind storming in the trees, and the black clouds flying over the moon. It frightened the black-fellows directly.

They stopped in their headlong speed, shouting together in their shrill voices, "The Bunyip! The Bunyip!" and they tumbled over one another in their hurry to get away from a place haunted, as they thought, by that wicked demon which they fear so much. At full speed they fled back to their camp, with the sound of Dot's cries, and the mysterious bellowing noise, following them on the breeze; and they never stopped running until they regained the light of their camp-fires. There they told the gins, in awe-struck voices, how it had been no kangaroo they had hunted, but the "Bunyip", who had pretended to be one. And the black gins' eyes grew wider and wider, and they made strange noises and exclamations, as they listened to the story of how the "Bunyip" had led the huntsmen to that dreadful place. How it had torn one of the dogs to pieces, and had leaped over the precipice into Dead Man's Gully, where it had cried like a piccaninny and bellowed like a bull. No one slept in the camp that night, and early next morning the whole tribe went away, being afraid to remain so near the haunt of the dreaded "Bunyip".

Dot saw the flight of the blacks in the dim distance and told the good news to the Kangaroo, who, however, was too exhausted to rejoice at their escape. She still lay where she had fallen, gasping, with her tongue hanging down from her mouth like that of a dog.

In vain Dot caressed her, and called her by endearing names. She lay quite still, as if unable to hear or feel. Dot's little heart swelled within her, and taking the poor animal's drooping head on her lap, she sat quite still and tearless; waiting in that solitude for her one friend to die—leaving her lonely and hopeless.

Presently she was startled by hearing a brisk voice: "Then it was a human piccaninny, after all! Well, my dear, what are you doing here?"

Dot turned her head without moving, and saw a little way behind her a brown bird on long legs, standing with its feet close together, with the self-satisfied air of a dancing master about to begin a lesson.

Dot did not care for any other creature in the bush just then but her Kangaroo, and the perky air of the bird annoyed her in her sorrow. Without answering, she bent her head closer down to that of her poor friend, to see if her eyes were still shut, and wondered if they would ever open and look bright and gentle again.

The little brown bird strutted with an important air to where it had a better view of Dot and her companion, and eyed them both in the same perky manner. "Friend Kangaroo's in a bad way," it said. "Why don't you do something sensible, instead of messing about with its head?"

"What can I do?" whimpered Dot.

*The Bittern helps Dot*

"Give it water, and damp its skin, of course," said the little bird, contemptuously. "What fools Humans are," it exclaimed to itself. "And I suppose you will tell me there is no water here, when all the time you are sitting on a spring."

"But I'm sitting on grass," said Dot, now fully attentive to the bird's remarks.

"Well, booby," sneered the bird, "and under the grass is wet moss, which, if you make a hole in it, will fill with water. Why, I'd do it myself, in a moment, only your claws are better suited for the purpose than mine. Set about it at once!" it said sharply.

In an instant Dot did what the bird directed, and thrust her little hands into the soft grass roots and moss, out of which water pressed, as if from a sponge. She had soon made a little hole, and the most beautiful clear water welled up into it at once. Then, in the hollows of her little hands, she collected it, and dashed it over the Kangaroo's parched tongue, and, further, instructed by the kindly though rude little bird, she had soon well wetted the suffering animal's fur. Gradually the breathing of the Kangaroo became less of an effort, her tongue moistened and returned to the mouth, and at last Dot saw with joy the brown eyes open, and she knew that her good friend was not going to die, but would get well again.

Whilst all this took place, the little brown bird stood on one leg, with its head cocked on one side, watching the exhausted Kangaroo's recovery with a comic expression of curiosity and conceit. When it spoke to Dot, it did so without any attempt at being polite, and Dot thought it the strangest possible creature, because it was really very kind in helping her to save the Kangaroo's life, and yet it seemed to delight in spoiling its kind-heartedness by its rudeness. Afterwards the Kangaroo told her that the little Bittern is a really tender-hearted fellow, but he has an idea that kindness in rather small creatures provokes the contempt of the big ones. As he always wants to be thought a bigger bird than he is, he pretends to be hard-hearted by being rough; consequently, nearly all the bush creatures simply regard him as a rude little bird, because bad manners are no proof of being grown-up; rather the contrary.

"How do you feel now?" asked the Bittern, as the Kangaroo

presently struggled up and squatted rather feebly on her haunches, looking about in a somewhat dazed way.

"I'm better now," said the Kangaroo, "but, dear me, how everything seems to dance up and down!" She shut her eyes, for she felt giddy.

"That was rather a good jump of yours," said the Bittern, patronizingly, as if jumps for life like that of Dot's Kangaroo were made every day, and he was a judge of them!

"Ah, I remember!" said the Kangaroo, opening her eyes again and looking round. "Where is Dot?"

"Umph, that silly!" exclaimed the Bittern, as Dot came forward, and she and the Kangaroo rejoiced over each other's safety. "Much good she'd have been to you with the blacks and their dogs after you, if we Bitterns hadn't played that old trick of ours of scaring them with our big voices. He, he, he!" it chuckled. "How they did run when we tuned up! They thought the Bunyip had got them this time. Didn't we laugh!"

"It was very good of you," said the Kangaroo gratefully, "and it is not the first time you have saved kangaroos by your cleverness. I didn't know you Bitterns were near, so I told Dot to make a noise in the hope of frightening them."

The Bittern was really touched by the Kangaroo's gratitude, and was delighted at being called clever, so it became still more ungracious. "You needn't trouble me with thanks," it said indifferently. "We didn't do it to save you, but for our own fun. As for that little stupid," it continued, with a nod of the head towards Dot, "her squeals were no more good than the squeak of a tree-frog in a Bittern's beak."

"But you were very kind," said Dot, "and showed me how to get water to save Kangaroo's life."

The Bittern was greatly pleased at this praise, and in consequence it got still ruder, and making a face at Dot, exclaimed, "Yah!" and stalked off. But when it had gone a few steps it turned round and said to the Kangaroo, roughly: "If you hop that way, keeping to the side of the sedges, and go half a dozen small hops beyond that white gum-tree, you'll find a little cave. It's dry and warm, and good enough for kangaroos." And without waiting for thanks for this last kind act, it spread its wings and flew away.

# Chapter Nine

THE Kangaroo, hopping very weakly, and little Dot trudging over the oozy ground, followed the Bittern's directions and found the cave, which proved a very snug retreat. Here they lay down together, full of happiness at their escape, and being worn out with fatigue and excitement, they were soon fast asleep.

The next day, before the sun rose, the Bittern visited the cave. "Hello, you precious lazy pair! I've been over there," and it tossed its beak in the direction of the blacks' camp. "They're off northward. Too frightened to stay. I thought you might like the news brought you, since you're too lazy to get it for yourselves!" and off it went again without saying good-bye.

"Now isn't he a kind little fellow?" said the Kangaroo. "That's his way of telling us that we are safe."

"Thanks, Bittern, thanks!" they both cried, but the creamy brown bird paid no attention to their gratitude: it seemed absorbed in looking for frogs on its way.

All that day the Kangaroo and Dot stayed near the cave, so that the poor animal might get quite well again. The Kangaroo said she did not know that part of the country, and so she had better get her legs again before they faced fresh dangers. Neither of them was so bright and merry as before. The weather was showery, and Dot kept thinking that perhaps she would never get home, now she had been so long away, and she kept remembering the time when the little boy was lost and everyone's sadness.

The Kangaroo, too, seemed melancholy.

"What makes you sad?" asked Dot.

"I am thinking of the last time before this that I was hunted. It was then I lost my baby kangaroo," she replied.

"Oh, you poor, dear thing!" exclaimed Dot, "and have you been hunted before last night?"

"Yes," said the Kangaroo, with a little weary sigh. "It was just a few days before I found you. White Humans did it that time."

"Tell me all about it," said Dot. "How did you escape?"

"I escaped then," said the Kangaroo, settling herself on her haunches to tell the tale, "in a way I could have done last night. But I will die sooner than do it again."

"Tell me," repeated Dot.

"There is not much to tell," said the Kangaroo. "My little Joey was getting quite big, and we were very happy. It was a lovely Joey. It was so strong, and could jump so well for its size. It had the blackest of little noses and hands and tail you ever saw, and big soft ears which heard more quickly than mine. All day long I taught it jumping, and we played and were merry from sunrise to sunset. Until that day I had never been sad, and I thought all the creatures must be wrong to say that in this beautiful world there could be such cruel beings as they said white Humans were. That day taught me I was wrong, and I know now that the world is a sad place because Humans make it so; although it was made to be a happy place. We were playing on the side of a plain that day, and our game was hide-and-seek in the long grass. We were having great fun, when suddenly little Joey said, 'strange creatures are coming, big ones'.

"I hopped up the stony rise that fringed the plain, and thought as I did so I could hear a new sound on the breeze. Joey hid in the grass, but I went boldly into the open on the hillside to see where the danger was. I saw, far off, Humans on their big animals that go so quickly, and directly I hopped into the open, they raised a great noise like the blacks did last night, and I could see by the movement of the grass that they had those dreadful dogs they teach to kill us: they are far worse than dingoes. Joey heard the shouting and bounded into my pouch, and I went off as fast as I could. It was a worse hunt than last night, for it was longer, and there was no darkness to help me. I gradually got ahead in the chase, and I knew if I were alone I could distance them all; for we had seen them a long way off. But little Joey was heavy, though not so heavy as you are, and in the long distance I began to feel weak, as I did last night.

"I knew if I tried to go on as we were, that those cruel Humans, sitting quietly on those big beasts (which have four legs and never get tired) would overtake us, and their dogs (which carry no weight and go so fast) would tear me down before their masters even arrived, for I was going gradually slower. So I asked Joey if I dropped him into a soft bush whether he would hide until I came back for him. It was our only chance. I had an idea that if I did that he would be safe—even if I got killed; as they would be more likely to follow me, and never think I had parted from my little Joey. So we did this, and I crossed a creek, which put the hounds off the scent, and I got away. In the dusk I came back again to find Joey, but he had gone, and I could not find a trace of him. All night and all day I searched, but I've never seen my Joey since," said the Kangaroo sadly, and Dot saw the tears dim her eyes.

Dot could not speak all she felt. She was so sorry for the Kangaroo, and so ashamed of being a Human. She realized too, how good and forgiving this dear animal was; how she had cared for her, and nearly died to save her life, in spite of the wrongs done to her by human beings.

"When I grow up," she said, "I will never let anyone hurt a bush creature. They shall all be happy where I am."

"But there are so many Humans. They're getting to be as many as kangaroos," said the animal reflectively, and shook her head.

# Chapter Ten

THE fourth day of Dot's wanderings in the bush dawned brightly. The sun arose in a sky all gorgeous in gold and crimson, and flashed upon a world glittering with dewy freshness. Sweet odours from the aromatic bush filled the air, and every living creature made what noise it could, to show its joy in being happy and free in the beautiful bush. Rich and gurgling came the note of the magpies, the jovial kookaburras saluted the sun with rollicking laughter, the crickets chirruped, frogs croaked in chorus, or solemnly "popped" in deep vibrating tones, like the ring of a woodman's axe. Every now and then came the shriek of the plover, or the shrill cry of the peewit; and gayer and more lively than all the others was the merry clattering of the big Bush Wagtail in the distance.

As soon as the Kangaroo heard the Bush Wagtail, she and Dot hurried away to find him. No Christy minstrel rattling his bones ever made a merrier sound. Click-i-ti-clack, clack, clack, clack, clack, click-i-ti-clack, he rattled away as fast as he could, just as if he hadn't a moment to waste for taking breath, and as if the whole lovely world was made for the enjoyment of Bush Wagtails.

When Dot and the Kangaroo found him, he was swaying about on a branch, spreading his big tail like a fan, and clattering gaily; but he stopped in surprise as soon as he saw his visitors.

After greetings, he opened the conversation by talking of the weather, so as to conceal his astonishment at seeing Dot and the Kangaroo together.

"Lovely weather after the rain," he said; "the showers were needed very much, for insects were getting scarce, and I believe grass was getting rank, and not very plentiful. There will be a green shoot in a few days, which will be very welcome to kangaroos. I heard about you losing your Joey—my cousin told me. I was very sorry; so sad. Ah, well, such things will happen in the bush to anyone. We were most fortunate in our brood; none of the chicks fell out of the nest, every one of them escaped the Butcher-birds and were strong of wing. They are all doing well in the world.'

Then the vivacious bird came a little nearer to the Kangaroo, and, dropping his voice said:

"But friend Kangaroo, I'm sorry to see you've taken up with Humans. You know I have quite set my face against them, although my cousin is intimate with the whole race. Take my word for it, they're most uncertain friends. Two kookaburras were shot last week, in spite of government protection. Fact!" And as the bird spoke he nodded his head warningly towards the place where Dot was standing.

"This little Human has been lost in our bush," said the Kangaroo. "One had to take care of her, you know."

"Of course, of course; there are exceptions to all rules," chattered the Wagtail. "And so this is really the lost little Human there has been such a fuss about!" added he, eyeing Dot, and making a long whistle of surprise. "My cousin told me all about it."

"Then your cousin, Willy Wagtail, knows her lost way," said the Kangaroo joyfully, and Dot came a little nearer in her eagerness to hear the good news.

"Of course he does," answered the bird. "There's nothing happens that he doesn't know. You should have hunted him up."

"I didn't know where to find him," said the Kangaroo, "and I got into this country, which is new to me."

"Why he is in the same part that he nested in last season. It's no distance off," exclaimed the Wagtail. "If you could fly, you'd be there almost directly!" Then the bird gave a long description of the way they were to follow to find his cousin Willy, and with many warm thanks the Kangaroo and Dot bade him adieu.

As they left the Bush Wagtail they could hear him singing this song, which shows what a merry, happy fellow he is:

*Click-i-ti, click-i-ti-clack!*
*Clack! clack! clack! clack!*
*Who could cry in such weather, 'alack!'*
*With a sky so blue, and a sun so bright,*
*Sing 'winter, winter, winter is back!'*
*Sportive in flight, chatter delight,*
*Click-i-ti, click-i-ti-clack!*
*I'm so glad that I have the knack*
*Of singing clack! clack! clack!*
*If you wish to be happy, just follow my track,*
*Take this for a motto, this for a code,*
*Sing 'winter, winter, winter is back!'*
*Leave care to a toad, and live* a la mode!
*Click-i-ti, click-i-ti-clack!*

They had no difficulty in following the wagtail's directions. They soon struck a creek they had been told to pursue to its end, and about noon they found themselves in very pretty country. It reminded Dot of the journey they had made to find the Platypus, for there were the same beautiful growths of ferns and shrubs. There were also great trailing creepers which hung down like ropes from the tops of the tall trees they had climbed. These rope-like coils of the creepers made capital swings, and often Dot clambered into one of the big loops and sat swinging herself to and fro, laughing and singing, much to the delight and amusement of the Kangaroo.

*Swing! swing! a bird on the wing*
*It is not more happy than I!*
*Stooping to earth, and seeking the sky.*
*Swing! swing! swing!*
*See how high upward I fly!*
*Here, midst the leaves I swing;*
*Then, as fast to my swing I cling,*
*Down I come from the sky!*
*Swing! swing! a bird on the wing*
*Is not more happy than I!*

Thus sang little Dot, tossing herself backwards and forwards, and the Kangaroo came to the conclusion that there was something very sweet about little Humans and that Dot was certainly quite as nice as a Joey Kangaroo.

In the middle of one of these little swinging diversions, a bird about the size of a pigeon, with the most wonderfully shiny plumage, flew to the tree on which Dot was swinging. Dot was so struck by the bird's beautiful blue-black glossy appearance, and its brightly contrasting yellow beak and legs, that she stopped swinging at once.

"You *are* a pretty bird!" she said.

"I am a Satin Bower-bird," it said. "We heard you singing, and we thought, therefore, that you probably enjoy parties, so I have come to invite you to one of our assemblies which will take place shortly. Friend Kangaroo, we know, is of a somewhat serious nature, but probably she will do us the pleasure of accompanying you to our little entertainment."

"I shall have great pleasure in doing so," said the Kangaroo. "I have not been at any of your parties for a long time. You know, I suppose, that I lost my little Joey very sadly?"

"We heard all about it," replied the Bower-bird in a tone of exaggerated, almost ridiculous sadness, for it was so anxious that the Kangaroo should think that it felt very deeply for her loss. "We were in the middle of a meeting at the time the Wallaby brought the news, and we were so sad that we nearly broke up our assembly. But it would have been a pity to do so, really, as the young birds enjoy themselves so much at the 'Bower of Pleasure'. But," said the Satin-bird, with a sudden change of tone from extreme sorrow to one of vivacious interest, "I must show you the way to the bower, or you will never find it."

Dot jumped down from the swing, and she and the Kangaroo, guided by the Satin-bird, made their way through some very thickly-grown bush. The bird was certainly right in saying that they would never have found the Bower of Pleasure without a guide. It was carefully concealed in the most densely-grown scrub. As they were pushing their way through a thicket of shrubs, before reaching the open space where the Satin-birds' bower was built, they heard an increasing noise of birds all talking to one another. The din of this chattering was enhanced considerably by the shrill sounds of tree-frogs and crickets, and the hubbub made Dot feel like the little Native Bear—as if her "head was empty".

"This will be a very pleasant party," said the Satin-bird, "there is plenty of conversation, so everyone's in a good humour."

*The Bower Birds*

"Do you think anyone is listening, or are they all talking?" inquired the Kangaroo timidly.

"Nobody would attempt to listen," answered the Satin-bird. "It would be impossible against the music of the tree-frogs and crickets, so everyone talks."

"I should tell the tree-frogs and crickets to be quiet," said Dot. "No one seems to care for their music."

"Oh, without music it would be very dull," explained the Satin-bird. "No one would care to talk. You understand, it would be awkward; someone might overhear what was said."

As the bird spoke the trio reached the place where the bower was situated.

Dot thought it a most curious sight. In the middle of an open space the birds had built a flooring of twigs, and upon that they had erected a bower about three feet high, also constructed of twigs interwoven with grass, and arranged so as nearly to meet at the top in an arched form.

"It's a new bower, and more commodious than our last," said the Satin-bird with an air of satisfaction. "What do you think of the decorations?"

In a temporary lull of the frog and cricket band and the conversation, Dot and the Kangaroo praised the bower and its decorations, and inquired politely how the birds had managed to procure such a collection of ornaments for their pleasure hall. Several young bower-birds came and joined in the chat, and Dot was surprised to see how different their plumage was from the satin blue-black of the old birds. These younger members of the community were of a greenish yellow colour, with dark pencillings on their feathers, and had no glossy sheen like their elders.

Each of them pointed out some ornament that it had brought with which to deck the bower. One had brought the pink feathers of a Galah, which had been stuck here and there amongst the twigs. Others had collected the delicate shells of land snails, and put them round about the entrance. But the birds that were proudest of their contributions were those who had picked up odds and ends at the camps of bushmen.

"That beautiful bright thing I brought from a camp a mile away," said a bird, indicating a tag from a cake of tobacco.

"But it isn't so pretty as mine," said another, pointing to the glass stopper of a sauce bottle.

"Or mine," chimed in another bird, as it claimed a bright piece of tin from a milk-can that was inserted in the twigs just above the entrance of the bower.

"Nonsense, children!" said a grave old Satin-bird. "Your trifles are not to be compared with that beautiful object I found today and arranged along the top of the bower. The effect is splendid!"

As he spoke, Dot observed that, twined amidst the topmost twigs of the construction was a strip of red flannel from an old shirt, a bedraggled red rag that must have been found in an extinct camp-fire, judging by its singed edges.

The day Dot had lost her way she had been threading beads, and she still had upon her finger a ring of the pretty coloured pieces of glass. She saw the old Satin-bird look at this ring longingly, so she pulled it off, and begged that it might be added to the other decorations. It was instantly given the place of honour—over the entrance and above the piece of milk-tin.

This gift from Dot caused an immediate flow of conversation, because every bird was pleased to have something to talk about. They all began to say how beautiful the beads were. "Quite too lovely!" said one. "What a charming little Human!" exclaimed another. "Just the finish that our bower required," was a general remark, and a great many kept exclaiming, "So tasteful!" "So sweet!" "How elegant!" "Exquisite!" "It's a love!" "It's a dear!" and so on. A great deal more was said, but the oldest bower-bird, thinking that all the adjectives were getting used up, told the frogs and crickets to start the music again, so as to keep the excitement going, and all further observations were drowned in the noise.

Presently the younger birds flew down to the bower, and began to play and dance. Like a troop of children, they ran round and round the bower, and to and fro through it, gleefully chasing each other. Then they would assemble in groups, and hop up and down, and dance to one another in what Dot thought a rather awkward fashion; but she was thinking of the elegance and grace of the Native Companions, who can make beautiful movements with their long legs and necks, whilst these little bower-birds are rather ungainly in their steps.

What amused her was to see how the young cock birds showed off to the little hens. They were conceited fellows, and only seemed happy when they had five or six little hens looking admiringly at their every movement. At such times they would dance and hop with great delight; and the little hens, in a circle round them, watched their hops and steps with absorbed interest. Immensely pleased with himself, the young dancer would fluff out his feathers, so as to look as big as possible, and after strutting about, would suddenly shoot out a leg and a wing, first on one side and then on the other, then spring high into the air, and do a sort of step dance when his feet touched the earth again. Endless were the tricks he resorted to, to show off his feathers and dancing to the best advantage; and the little hens watched it all with silent intentness.

In the meantime, the frogs and crickets stopped to rest, and Dot could hear the conversation of some of the old birds perched near her. A little party of elderly hens were discussing the young birds who were dancing at the bower.

"I must say I don't admire that new step which is becoming so popular amongst the young birds," said one elderly hen; and all her companions rustled their feathers, closed their beaks tightly, and nodded their heads in various ways. One said it was "rough", another that it was "ungainly", and others that it was "unmannerly".

"As for manners," said the first speaker, "the bower-birds of this day can't be said to have any!" And all her companions chorused, "No, indeed!"

"In my young day," continued the elderly hen, and all the group were sighing, "Ah, in our young days!" when a young hen perched on a bough above them, and interrupted pertly, "Dear me, can't you good birds find anything more interesting to talk about than ancient history?" At this the group of gossips whispered angrily to one another, "Minx!" "Hussy!" "Wild cat!" etc., and the rude young bird flew back to her companions.

"What I object to most in young birds," said another elderly hen, "is their appearance. Some of them do nothing all day but preen their feathers. Look at the over-studied arrangements of their wing flights, and the affected exactness of their tail feathers! One looks in vain for sweetness and simplicity in the present-day young bower-birds."

"Even that is better than the newer fashion of scarcely preening the feathers at all," observed yet another of the group. "Many of the young birds take no pride in their feathers whatever, but devote all their time to studying the habits of out-of-the-way insects." A chorus of disapproval from all present supported this remark. "Studies that interfere with a young hen's appearance should not be permitted," said one bird.

"What is the good of knowing all about insects, when we live on berries and fruit?" asked another.

"The sight of insects gives one the creeps!" said a third.

"I am thankful to say all my little hens care for nothing beyond playing at the Bower and preening their feathers," said an affectionate bower-bird mother. "They get a deal of attention paid to them."

"No young Satin-bird would look at a learned little bower-hen," said the bird who had first objected to untidy and studious young hens. "For my part, I never allow a chick of mine even to mention insects, unless they are well-known beetles!"

Dot thought this chattering very stupid, so she went round a bush to where the old fathers of the bower-birds were perched. They were grave old fellows, arrayed in their satin blue-black plumage, and she found them all, more or less, in a grumbling humour.

"Birds at our time of life should not have to attend parties," said several, and Dot wondered why they came. "How are you, old neighbour?" said one to another. "Terribly bored!" was the reply. "How long must we stay, do you think?" asked another. "Oh, until these young fools have finished amusing themselves," answered his friend. The only satin-birds who seemed to Dot to be interested in one another, were some engaged in discussing the scarcity of berries and the wrongs done to bower-birds by white Humans destroying the wild fig and lillipilli-trees. This grievance, and the question as to what berries or figs agreed best with each old bower-bird's digestion, were the only topics discussed with any animation.

Dot soon tired of listening to the birds, and returned to the Kangaroo, who asked her if she cared to stay any longer. The little girl said she had seen and heard enough, and, judging by this one, she didn't care for parties.

"Neither do I," whispered the Kangaroo. "They make me feel tired; and, somehow, they seem to remind one of everything one knows that's sad, in spite of all the gaiety."

"Is it gay?" inquired Dot, hesitating a little in her speech, for she had felt rather dull and miserable.

"Well, everyone says it's gay, and there is always a deal of noise, so I suppose it is," answered the Kangaroo.

"I'd rather be in your pouch, so let us go away," entreated Dot; and they left the bower place without any of the birds noticing their departure, for they were all busy gossiping, or discussing the great berry or digestion questions.

It was towards evening when they reached an open plain, and here they met an Emu. As both Dot and the Kangaroo were thirsty, they asked the Emu the way to a waterhole or tank.

"I am going to a tank now," replied the Emu. "Let us proceed together."

"Do you think it will be safe to drink tonight?" inquired the Kangaroo anxiously.

"Well, to tell the truth," said the Emu lightly, "it is likely to be a little difficult. There is a somewhat strained feeling between the white Humans and ourselves just now. In consequence, we have to resort to a little strategy on our visits to the tanks, and we avoid eating anything tempting left about at camping places."

"Are they laying poison for *you*?" asked the Kangaroo in horrified tones.

"They are doing something of the kind, we think," answered the Emu airily, "for some of us have had most unpleasant symptoms after picking up morsels at camping grounds. Several have died. We were quite surprised, for hitherto there had been no better cure for Emu indigestion than wire nails, hoop iron, and preserved milk cans. The worst symptoms have yielded to scraps of barbed wire in my own case. But these Emus died in spite of all remedies."

"But I heard," said the Kangaroo, "that Emus were protected by the Government. I never understood why."

"We are protected," said the huge bird, "because we form part of the Australian Arms."

"So do we," said the Kangaroo, "but we are not protected."

"True," said the bird, "but the Humans can make some money out of you when you are dead, whereas we serve no purpose at all, excepting alive, when we add charm to the scenery; and, moreover, each of our eggs will make a pound cake. But the time will come, friend, when there will be neither Emu nor Kangaroo for Australia's Arms; no creature will be left to represent the land but the Bunny Rabbit and the Sheep."

"I hate sheep!" said the Kangaroo. "They eat all our grass."

"You have not studied them as we have," answered the Emu. "They are most entertaining. We have great fun with them, and we've learnt some capital sheep games from those dogs Humans drive them with. It's really exciting to drive a big mob, when they want to break and scatter. We were chasing them, here and there, all over the plain today."

"I don't like sheep!" said Dot. "They are so stupid."

"So they are," agreed the Emu, "and that is what puzzles me. What is it about the sight of sheep that excites one so? When one gets into a big flock, one has to dance, one can't help oneself. We had a great dance in a flock today, and the lambs would get under our feet, so I'm sorry to say a good many of them were killed."

"Men will certainly kill you, if you do that," said Dot.

"We know it," chuckled the Emu; "that is why the tank is not quite safe just now. But this evening I will show you a new plan by which to learn if Humans are camped at a tank, or not. We have played the trick with great success for several nights."

Conversing thus, the Emu, the Kangaroo, and Dot wandered on until the Emu requested them to wait for a few minutes, whilst it peeped at the tank, which was still a long way off.

It presently returned and said that it felt quite suspicious, because everything looked so clear and safe. "From this point of high ground," said the bird, "you can watch our proceedings. I will now give the signal and return to my post here."

The Emu then ran at a great pace along the edge of the plain, and emitted a strange rattling cry. After disappearing from sight for a time, it returned hurriedly to where Dot and her friend were waiting.

"Now, see!" said the Emu, nodding at the distant side of the plain.

Dot's eyes were not so keen of sight as those of an Emu; but she thought she could see something like a little cloud of dust, far, far away across the dry brown grass of the plain. Soon she was quite sure that the little cloud was advancing towards her side of the plain, and in the direction of the tank. As it came nearer she could see the bobbing heads of Emus, popping up above the dust, and she could see some of the birds running round the little cloud.

"What is the cause of all that dust?" she asked the Emu.

"Sheep!" it answered with a merry chuckle.

"But what are the Emus doing with the sheep?" asked Dot and the Kangaroo, now fully interested in the Emu's manoeuvre.

"They are driving them to water at the tank," said the bird, highly delighted with the scheme. "The sheep will soon know that they are near water, and will go to it without driving. Then we shall watch, and if they quietly drink and scatter, it will be safe for us, but if they see anything unusual and break, and run—well, we shan't drink at the tank tonight. There will be Humans and dogs there, and we don't cultivate their society just now."

"Really, that is the cleverest thing I have heard for a long time," said the Kangaroo, full of admiration for the trick. "How did you jump to that conclusion?"

"The idea sprang upon us," answered the Emu, with an immense hop in the air, and a dancing movement when it came to the ground again. "Dear me!" it exclaimed, "the sight of those sheep is beginning to excite me, and I can hardly keep still! I wonder what there is so exciting about sheep!"

Dot could now see the advancing flock of sheep, with their attendant mob of Emus, quite well. The animals had got scent of the water, and with contented bleatings were slowly moving with a rippling effect across the dusty plain. The mob of Emus soon left the sheep to go their own way, and grouped in a cluster, watched, with bobbing heads, every movement of the flock.

Dot, the Kangaroo, and the Emu looked towards the tank with silent interest. "I'm stationed here," whispered the bird, "to give a

*The Emus hunting the Sheep*

warning in case there is any danger in this direction. Emus are posted all round the tank on the same duty."

Dot could see the whole scene well, for beyond a few low shrubs on the opposite side of the sheet of water, there was no sheltering bush near the great tank which had been excavated on the bare plain.

Onward came the sheep, and quite stationary in the distance remained the Emu mob. Just as the first sheep were descending the deep slope of the tank, a Plover rose from amongst the bushes with a shrill cry. The Emu started at the sound, and whispered to the Kangaroo: "There'll be no drink tonight. Watch!"

The cry of the Plover seemed to arrest the advance of the timid sheep. They waited in a closely-packed flock, looking around. But presently the old leader gave a deep bleat, and they moved forwards towards the water. "Shriek! Shriek!" cried the Plover from the bushes, screaming as they rose and flew away; and suddenly the flock of sheep broke and hurried back to the open plain. At the same instant Dot could hear the sharp barking of a sheep-dog, a noise that produced an instant effect on the creatures she was with. With lightning speed the Kangaroo had popped her into her pouch and was hopping away, and the Emu was striding with its long legs as fast as it could for the cover of the bush.

Just as they entered the bush shelter, Dot peeped out of the pouch, across the plain, and could see the mob of Emus in a cloud of dust, running, and almost out of sight.

When they had reached a place of safety, the friendly Emu bid the Kangaroo and Dot good-night. "We shall have to go thirsty tonight," it said, "but there will be a heavy dew, and the grass will be wet enough to cool one's mouth. That pretty trick of ours was such a success that it is almost worth one's while to lose one's drink in proving it." Turning to Dot, it said, "You will be able to tell the big Humans that we Emus are not such fools as they think, and that we find their flocks of silly sheep most useful and entertaining animals."

Chuckling to itself, the Emu strode off, leaving Dot and the Kangaroo to pass another night in the solitude of the bush.

# Chapter Eleven

THE next day they travelled a long distance. At about noon they came to a part of the country which the Kangaroo said she knew well. "But we must be careful," she added, "as we are very near Humans in this part."

As Dot was tired (for she had had to walk much more than usual) the Kangaroo suggested that she should rest at the pretty spot they had reached, whilst she herself went in search of Willy Wagtail. Dot had to promise the Kangaroo over and over again, not to leave the spot during her absence. She was afraid lest the little girl should get lost, like her little Joey.

After many farewells, and much hopping back to give Dot warnings and make promises of returning soon, the Kangaroo went in search of Willy Wagtail; and the little girl was left all alone.

Dot looked for a nice shady nook, in which to lie down and rest; and she found the place so cheerful and pretty, that she was not afraid of being alone. She was in the hollow of an old watercourse. It was rather like an English forest glade, it was so open and grassy; and here and there were pretty shrubs, and little hillocks and hollows. At first Dot thought that she would sit on the branch of a huge tree that had but recently fallen, and lay forlornly clothed in withered leaves; but opposite to this dead giant of the bush was a thick shrub with a decayed tree-stump beside it, that made a nice sheltered corner which she liked better. So Dot laid herself down there, and in a few minutes she was fast asleep; though, as she dropped off into the land of dreams, she thought how wonderfully quiet that little glade was, and felt somewhat surprised to find no bush creatures to keep her company.

Some time before Dot woke, her dreams became confused and strange. There seemed to be great crowds in them, and the murmur of many voices talking together. As she gradually awakened, she realized that the voices were real, and not a part of her dreams. There was a great hubbub, a fluttering of wings, and rustling of leaves and grass. Through all this confusion, odd sentences became clear to her drowsy senses. Such phrases as, "You'd better perch here!" "This isn't your place!" "Go over there!" "No, no, I'm sure I'm right! The Welcome Swallow says so." "Has anyone gone for the Opossum?" "He says the court ought to be held at night!" "Don't make such a noise or you will wake the prisoner." "Who is to be the judge?" This last inquiry provoked such a noise of diverse opinions, that Dot became fully awake, and sitting up, gazed around with eyes full of astonishment.

When she had fallen asleep there had not been a creature near her; but now she was literally hemmed in on every side by birds and small animals. The branches of the fallen tree were covered with a feathered company, and in the open space between it and Dot's nook, was a constantly increasing crowd of larger birds, such as cranes, plover, duck, turkey-buzzards, black swan, and amongst them a great grave Pelican. The animals were few, and apparently came late. There was a little timid Wallaby, a Bandicoot, some Kangaroo Rats, a shy Wombat, who grumbled about the daylight, as also did a Native Bear and an Opossum, who were really driven to the gathering by a bevy of screaming parrots.

Dot was wide awake at once with delight. Nearly every creature she had ever heard of seemed to be present, and the brilliant colours of the parrots and parakeets made the scene as gay as a rainbow in a summer noonday sky.

"Oh, you darlings!" she said. "How good of you all to come and see me!"

This greeting from Dot caused an instant silence amongst the creatures, and she could not help seeing that they looked very un-

*The court of animals*

comfortable. There was soon a faint whispering from bird to bird, which rose higher and higher, until Dot made out that they were all saying, "She ought to be told!" "You tell her!" "No, you tell her yourself, it's not my business!" And every bird—for it was the birds who by reason of their larger numbers took the lead in the proceedings—seemed to be trying to shift an unpleasant task upon its neighbours.

Presently the solemn Pelican waddled forward and stood before Dot, saying to the assemblage, "I will explain our presence." Addressing the little girl, it said: "We are here to place you on trial for the wrongs we Bush creatures have suffered from the cruelties of white Humans. You will meet with all fairness in your trial, as the proceedings will be conducted according to the custom of your own courts of justice. The Welcome Swallow, having built its nest for three successive seasons under the eaves of the Gabblebabble Court House, is deeply learned in human law business, and will instruct us how to proceed. Your conviction will, therefore, leave you no room for complaint so far as your trial is concerned."

All the birds clapped their wings in applause at the conclusion of this speech, and the Pelican was told by the Welcome Swallow that he should plead as prosecutor.

"What do you mean by 'plead as prosecutor'?" asked the Pelican gravely.

"You've got to get the prisoner convicted as guilty, whether she is or not," answered the Swallow, making a dart at a mosquito, which it ate with relish.

"Oh!" said the Pelican doubtfully; and all the creatures looked at one another as if they didn't quite understand the justice of the arrangement.

"But," said the Pelican, hesitating a little, "suppose I don't think the prisoner guilty? She seems very small and harmless."

"That doesn't matter at all, you've got to get her made out as guilty by the jury. It's good human law," snapped the Swallow, and all the creatures said, "*Oh!*" "Now for the defence," said the Swallow briskly. "There ought to be someone for that. Who is friendly with the king?"

"Who's the king?" asked all the creatures breathlessly.

"He's a bigger Human than the rest, and everybody's business is his business, so he's always going to law."

"I know," said the Magpie, and she piped out six bars of "God Save the King."

"You are the one for the defence!" said the Swallow, quite delighted, as were all the other creatures, at the Magpie's accomplishment. "You must save the prisoner from the jury finding her guilty."

"But," objected the Magpie, "how can I, when only last fruit season my brother, and two sisters, and six cousins were shot just because they ate a few grapes?"

"That doesn't matter! You've got to get her off, I tell you!" said the Swallow, irritably. "Go over there and ask her what you are to say." So the Magpie flew over to Dot's side, and she at once began to teach it the rest of "God Save the King".

"I like this game," Dot presently said to the Magpie.

"Do you?" said the Magpie with surprise. "It seems to me very slow, and there's no sense in it."

"Why are the birds all perching together over there?" asked Dot, pointing to a branch of the dead tree, "since they all hate one another and want to get away. The Galahs have pecked the Butcher-bird twice in five minutes, the Peewit keeps quarrelling with the Soldier-bird, and none of them can bear the English Sparrow."

"The Swallow says that's the jury," answered the Magpie. "Their business is to do just what they like with you when all the talking is done, and whether they find you guilty or not, will depend on if they are tired, or hungry, or feel cross; or if the trial lasts only a short time, and they are pleased with the grubs that will be brought them presently."

"How funny," said Dot, not a bit alarmed at all these preparations for her trial, for she loved all the creatures so much, that she could not think that any of them wished to hurt her.

"If this is human law," said the Magpie, "it isn't funny at all; it is mad, or wicked. Fancy my having to defend a Human!"

At this point of the conversation, the ill-feeling amongst the jury broke out into open fighting, because the English Sparrow was a foreigner, and they said it would certainly sympathize with the humans who had brought it to Australia. This was just an excuse to get rid of it. The Sparrow said that it wanted to go out of the jury, and had never wished to belong to it, and flew away joyfully. Then all the rest of the jury grumbled at the good luck of the Sparrow in getting out of the trial—for they could see it picking up grass seed and enjoying itself greatly, whilst they were all crowded together on one branch, and were feeling hungry before the trial had ever begun.

There was great suspense and quiet while the judge was being chosen. Although Dot had eaten the berries of understanding, it was generally considered that, to be quite fair, the judge must be able to understand human talk; and, amidst much clapping of wings, a large white Cockatoo was appointed.

The Cockatoo lost no time in clambering "into position" on the stump near Dot. "You're quite sure you understand human talk?" said the little Wallaby to the Cockatoo. It was the first remark he had made, for he had been quite bewildered by all the noise and fuss.

"My word! yes," replied the Cockatoo, who had been taught in a public refreshment-room. Then, thinking that he would give a display of his learning, he elevated his sulphur crest and gabbled off, "Go to Jericho! Twenty to one on the favourite! I'm your man! Now then, ma'am; hurry up, don't keep the coach waiting! Give 'um their 'eds, Bill! So long! Ta-ra-ra, boom-di-ay! God save the King!"

All the creatures present looked gravely at Dot, to see what effect this harangue in her own language would have upon her, and were somewhat surprised to see her holding her little sides, and rolling about with laughter.

The Cockatoo was quite annoyed at Dot's amusement. He fluffed out all his feathers, and let off a scream that could have been heard a quarter of a mile away. This seemed to impress everyone with his importance, and the whole Court became attentive to the proceedings.

At this moment the Swallow skimmed overhead, and having caught the words "God save the King", called out, "That's the way to do it! Keep that up!" And the Cockatoo, thinking that the Swallow meant him to scream still more, set up another yell, which he continued until everyone felt deafened by the noise.

"We have chosen quite the right judge," said an elegant blue

*The Cockatoo Judge*

crane to a wild duck; "he will make himself heard and respected." Whereat the Cockatoo winked at the Crane, and said, "You bet I will!"

The Pelican now advanced to the space before the stump, and there was a murmur of excitement, because it was about to open the trial by a recital of wrongs done to the Bush creatures by white humanity.

Dot could not realize that she was being tried seriously, and was delighted that the Pelican had come nearer to her stump, so that she had a better view of him. She thought him such an old, odd-looking bird, with his big bald head, and gigantic beak. She could not help thinking that his beak must be too heavy for him, and asked if he would like to rest it on the stump. The Pelican did not understand Dot's kindness, and gave her a look of offended dignity that was quite withering, so Dot did not speak to him again; but she longed to feel if the bag of skin that drooped under his beak had anything in it. The Pelican's legs seemed to Dot to be too frail and short to bear such a big bird, not to mention the immense beak; and, when the creature stood on one leg only, she laughed; whereat the Pelican gave her another offended look, which effectually prevented their becoming friends.

The Pelican was beginning to open his beak to speak (and, being such a large beak, opening it took some time), when the Welcome Swallow fussed into court, and said that "nothing could be done until they had some horsehair!"

This interruption, and the Swallow's repeated assurance that no human trial of importance could take place without horsehair, set all the creatures chattering with astonishment and questions. Some said the Swallow was joking; others said that it was making senseless delays, and that night would fall before they could bring the prisoner to justice. There was much grumbling on all sides, and complaints of hunger, and the jury began to clamour for the grubs that they had been promised, at which the Magpie whispered to Dot that she certainly would be found guilty. The fact was now quite clear to the jury before the trial began.

But the Swallow persisted that they must have horsehair.

"What tor?" asked everyone, sulkily.

"Don't you see for yourselves," squeaked the Swallow, excitedly; "the judge looks like a Cockatoo."

"Well, of course he does," said all the creatures. "He is a Cockatoo, so he looks like one!"

"Yes," cried the Swallow, "but you must stick horsehairs on his head. Human justice must be done with horsehair. The prisoner won't believe the Cockatoo is a judge without. Good gracious!" exclaimed the Swallow, "just look! The prisoner is scratching the judge's poll! We really *must* have horsehair!"

Dot, seeing the Swallow's indignation, drew away from the stump, and the Cockatoo tried to look as if he had never seen her before, and as if the idea of having his poll scratched by the prisoner was one that could never have entered his head.

"But if we do put horsehair on the Cockatoo's head," argued the creatures, "what will it do?"

"It will impress the prisoner," said the Swallow.

"How?" they all asked, curiously.

"Because the Cockatoo won't look like a Cockatoo," replied the Swallow with exasperation.

"Then what will he look like?" asked every creature in breathless excitement.

"He won't look like any creature that ever lived," retorted the Swallow.

Perfect silence followed this explanation, for every bird and animal was trying to understand human sense and reason. Then the smallest Kangaroo Rat broke the stillness.

"If," said the Kangaroo Rat, "only a little horsehair can do that, surely the prisoner can imagine the judge isn't a Cockatoo, without our having to wait for the horsehair. Let's go on with the trial."

This idea was received with applause, and the Swallow flew off in a huff; whilst the Kookaburra, on a tree near the court, softly laughed to himself.

Once more the Pelican took up his position to open the trial. The Cockatoo puffed himself out as big as he could, fluffed out his cheek feathers, and half-closed his eyes. His solemnly attentive attitude won the admiration of all the court, and the absence of horsehair was not felt by anyone. The Welcome Swallow, having got over its ill-temper, returned to help the proceedings; and the jury all put their heads under their wings and went to sleep.

"Fire away!" screamed the Cockatoo, and the trial began.

"My duty is a most painful one," said the Pelican; "for" ("whereas," said the Swallow) "the prisoner known" ("named and described," added the Swallow), "as Dot is now before you" ("to be tried, heard, determined, and adjudged," gabbled the Swallow) "on a charge of cruelty" ("and feloniously killing and slaying," prompted the Swallow) "to birds and animals," ("the term not applying to horse, mare, pony, bull, ox, dog, cat, heifer, steer, calf, mule, ass, sheep, lamb, hog, pig, sow, goat, or other domestic animal," interposed in one breath the Swallow, quoting the Cruelty to Animals Act) "she is" ("hereby," put in the Swallow) "brought to trial on" ("divers," whispered the Swallow) "charges" ("hereinafter," said the Swallow), "to be named and described by the" ("aforesaid," interjected the Swallow) "birds and animals" ("hereinbefore mentioned," stated the Swallow), "the said animals being denizens of the bush" ("and in no wise relating to horse, mare, pony, bull, ox——" began the Swallow again, when the Cockatoo raised his crest, and screamed out: *"Stop that, I tell you!"* and the Pelican continued stating the charge.) "Bush law" ("enacts," said the Swallow) "that" ("whereas," prompted the Swallow) "all individual rights" ("whatsoever," put in the Swallow) "shall be according to the statute Victoria——"

"Victoria! Twenty to one against the field," shouted the judge.

"Between you two," said the Pelican, looking angrily at the Swallow and the Cockatoo, "I've forgotten everything I was going to say! I shan't go on!"

"Never mind," said the Swallow cheerfully, "you've said quite enough, and no one has understood a word of the charge, so it's all right. Now then, for the witnesses."

As the Swallow spoke, there was a great disturbance amongst the creatures. The swans, ducks, cranes, and waterfowl, besides honey-suckers, and many other birds, were all fanning the air with their wings, and crying, "Turn him out!" "Disgusting!" "I never heard of such a thing in my life!" "The smell of it always gives me a headache!"

*The Pelican opens the case*

And there was such a noise that the jury all woke up, and Dot covered her ears with her hands. The Cockatoo, seeing Dot's distress at the screams and hubbub, and thinking that she wanted to say something, but could not make herself heard in the general riot, decided to speak for her; so he screamed louder than all the rest, and shouted: "Apples, oranges, pears, lemonade, cigarettes, *and* cigars! I say, what's the row?"

When quiet was restored, it was explained that the Opossum had brought into court a pouch full of gum-leaves, which it was eating. It had also given some to the Native Bear, and Wallaby, and in consequence the whole air was laden with the odour of eucalyptus.

"Oh, dear!" said Dot, "it smells just like when I have a cold!"

"Eating eucalyptus leaves in court is contempt of court," cried the Swallow; and everyone echoed, "Contempt of court! Contempt of court! Turn them out!"

"But they are witnesses," objected the Pelican.

"That doesn't matter!" shouted the Waterfowl. "It's a disgusting smell! Turn them out!"

"Hurrah!" shouted the Wallaby, as it leaped off. "What luck!" laughed the Opossum, as it cleared into the nearest tree. "I am glad," sighed the Koala, as it slowly moved away; "that trial made my head feel empty."

"Well, there go three of the most important witnesses," grumbled the Pelican.

"My eye, what a spree," said the judge.

A Galah amongst the jury, wishing to be thought intelligent, inquired what charge the Wallaby, Native Bear, and Opossum were to bear witness to.

"It is a matter of skins, included in the fur rugs clause, and the wickedness known as 'Sport'," answered the Pelican.

Whilst the Pelican was making this explanation, the judge, who had been longing to have his poll scratched again, sidled up to Dot, and whispered softly to her, "Scratch Cockie!" But, just as he was enjoying the delicious sensation Dot's fingers produced amongst his neck feathers, as he held his head down, the Pelican caught sight of the proceeding. The Pelican said nothing, but stared at the judge with an eye of such astonishment and stern contempt, that the Cockatoo instantly remembered that he was a judge, and, getting into a proper attitude, said hastily: "Advance, Australia! Who's the next witness?" And again the Kookaburra laughed to himself on the tree.

"Fur first!" exclaimed a white ibis. "Call the Platypus!"

"The Platypus won't come!" cried the Kangaroo Rat.

"Well, I never!" exclaimed the judge.

"It says that if a court is held at all, it should be conducted by the representative of Antediluvian custom, the most ancient and learned creatures, such as the Iguana, the Snake, the Ornithorhynchus Paradoxus. That it would prefer to associate with the meanest Troglodite, rather than appear amongst the present company. I understood it to say," continued the Kangaroo Rat, "that real law could only be understood by those deeply learned in fossils."

" 'Pon my word!" ejaculated the judge. "Shiver my timbers! What blooming impudence!"

"Oh, you naughty bird to use such words!" exclaimed Dot. But all the court murmured, "How clever!" and the Cockatoo was pleased.

"Native Cat, next!" shouted the white Ibis. But at the first mention of the Native Cat, nearly every bird, and all the small game, prepared to get away.

"Why don't you call the Dingo at once?" laughed the Kookaburra, who was really keeping guard over Dot, although she did not know it. "Humans kill Dingoes."

"The Dingo! The Dingo!" every creature repeated in horror and consternation; and they all looked about in fear, while the Kookaburra chuckled to himself at all the stir his words had made.

"It's quite true that animals and birds kill one another," said the Magpie, who thought he ought to say something in Dot's defence, as that was his part of the trial, "therefore it is the same nature that makes Humans kill us. If it is the nature of Humans to kill, the same as it is the nature of birds and animals to kill, where is the sense and justice of trying the prisoner for what she can't help doing?"

"Good!" said the Welcome Swallow; "argued like a lawyer."

At this unexpected turn of the trial, the judge softly whistled to himself, "Pop Goes the Weasel".

"Don't talk to us about nature and justice and sense," replied the Pelican, contemptuously. "This is a court of law; we have nothing to do with any of them!"

The court all cheered at this reply, and Magpie subsided in the sulks.

"Call the Kangaroo!" cried the white Ibis.

"It's no good," jeered the Kookaburra. "Kangaroo and Dot are great friends. She won't come if you called——"

"Till all's blue!" interrupted the judge, and he went on with "Pop Goes the Weasel". This news caused a buzz of excitement. Everyone was astounded that the Kangaroo, who had the heaviest grievances of all, wouldn't appear against the prisoner.

"Is it possible," said the Pelican, addressing the Kookaburra in slow, stern accents, "is it possible that the Kangaroo has forgiven all her grievances?"

"All," said the Kookaburra.

"The hunting?" asked the Pelican.

"Yes," answered the Kookaburra.

"The rugs?"

"Yes."

"The boots?"

"Yes."

"And," said the Pelican, still more solemnly and slowly, while all the court listened in breathless attention, "and has she forgiven *Kangaroo-tail soup*?"

"Yes, she's forgiven that, too!" answered the Kookaburra cheerfully.

"Then," said the Pelican, hotly, "I throw up the case," and he spread his huge black wings, and flapped his way up into the sky and away.

"What a go!" said the judge; and he might have said more, only Dot could not hear anything on account of the racket and confusion. The trial had failed, and every creature was making all the noise it could, and preparing to hurry away. In the middle of the turmoil, Dot's Kangaroo bounded into the open space, panting with excitement and delight.

"Dot! Dot!" she cried. "I've found Willy Wagtail, and he knows your way! Come along at once!" And, putting Dot in her pouch, the Kangaroo leaped clean over the judge and carried her off.

*The Kangaroo carries Dot out of court*

# Chapter Twelve

ALTHOUGH the Kangaroo was longing to hear the reason why so many bush creatures had collected round Dot whilst she was away, she was too anxious to carry her to Willy Wagtail before nightfall to wait and inquire what had happened. Dot, too, was so excited at hearing that her way home had been found, that she could only think of the delight of seeing her father and mother again. So the Kangaroo had hopped until she was tired and needed rest, before they spoke. Then Dot described the trial, and made the Kangaroo laugh about the Cockatoo judge, but she did not say how it had all ended because the Kangaroo had forgiven Dot for Humans making rugs of her fur, boots of her skin, and soup of her tail. She was afraid of hurting her feelings by mentioning such delicate subjects. The Kangaroo never noticed that anything was left out, because she was bursting to relate her interview with Willy Wagtail.

She told Dot how she had found Willy Wagtail near his old haunt; how that gossiping little bird had told all the news of the Gabblebabble town and district in ten minutes, and how he had said he believed he knew Dot by sight, and that if such were the case, he would show Dot and the Kangaroo the way to the little girl's home. Then Dot and the Kangaroo hurried on their way again, the little girl sometimes running and walking to rest the kind animal, and sometimes being carried in that soft cosy pouch that had been her cradle and carriage for all those days.

It was quite dusk by the time they arrived at a sliprail fence, and heard a little bird singing, "Sweet pretty creature! Sweet pretty creature!"

"That is Willy Wagtail making love," said the Kangaroo, with a humorous twinkle in her quiet eyes. "Peep round the bush," she said to Dot, "and you'll see them spooning."

Dot glanced through the branches, and saw two wagtails, who looked very smart in their black coats and white waistcoats, sitting on two posts of the fence a little way off. They were each pretending that their long tails were too heavy to balance them properly, and they seemed to be always just saving themselves from toppling off their perch. Occasionally, Willy would dart into the air, to show what an expert in flying he was; he would shoot straight upwards, turn a double somersault backwards, and wing off in the direction one least expected. Afterwards he would return to his post as calm and cool as if he had done nothing surprising, and say, "Pretty pretty Chip-pi-ti-chip!" that name meaning the other wagtail. Then Chip-pi-ti-chip showed off *her* flying, and they both said to one another, "Sweet pretty creature!"

At the sound of Dot and the Kangaroo's approach, Chip-pi-ti-chip hid herself in a tree, and Willy Wagtail, not knowing who was disturbing them, scolded angrily; but when he saw the Kangaroo and the little girl, he gave them the most cordial greeting, and wobbled about on a rail as if he must tumble off every second.

"This is Dot," said the Kangaroo, a little anxiously, and rather breathlessly with the speed she had made.

"Just as I had expected!" exclaimed Willy Wagtail, with a jerk of his tail which nearly sent him headlong off the rail. "I should know you anywhere, little Human, though you do look a bit different. You want preening," he added.

This last remark was in allusion to Dot's appearance, which certainly was most untidy and dirty, for, beyond an occasional lick from the Kangaroo, she had been five days without being tidied and cleaned.

"I couldn't do it better," said the Kangaroo apologetically.

"It doesn't matter at all," said Dot, putting her tangled curls back from her eyes.

"Well, I know where you live!" gabbled off the Wagtail. "It's the second big paddock from here, if you follow the belt of the she-oak trees over there. It's a house just like those things in Gabblebabble township. There's a yellow sheep-dog, who's very good tempered, and a black one that made a snap at my tail the other day. There is an old grey cart horse, an honest fellow, but rather dull; and a bay mare who is much better company. There is a little red cow who is a great friend of mine, and she had a calf a few days before you were lost. Dear me!" exclaimed the gossiping bird, "what a fuss there has been these five days over trying to find you! I've been over there every day to see the sight. Such a lot of Humans! And such horses! I enjoyed myself immensely, and made a lot of friends amongst the horses, but I didn't care so much for the dogs; I thought them a nasty quarrelsome lot.

"I went with the whole turnout to see the search. Goodness, the distances they went, and the noise and the big fires they made! It *was* exciting fun! They brought over some black Humans—'Trackers' they are called, at least the Mounted Troopers' horses told me so (my word! the troopers' horses are jolly fellows!). Well, these black trackers went in front of each party just like dogs, with their heads to the ground, and they turned over every leaf and twig, and said if a Human, a horse or a kangaroo had broken it or been that way, they would have found your track fast enough. But one evening it came to an end quite suddenly, and weren't they all surprised! I heard from a trooper's horse — (such a nice horse he was!)—that the trackers and white Humans said it was just as if you had disappeared into the sky! There was just a bit of your fur on a bush, and nothing anywhere else but a kangaroo's trail. No one could make it out."

"That was when I took you in my pouch!" exclaimed the Kangaroo.

"Now," said the Wagtail, "most of them have given up the search. Just this evening Dot's father and a few other Humans came back, and the yellow sheep-dog told me the last big party is to start at noon tomorrow, and after that there will be no more attempt to find Dot. Only the sheep-dog said he heard his master say he would go on hunting alone, until he found her body. I haven't been over there today," wound up the bird, "they are all so miserable and tired, it gave me the blues yesterday."

"What are we to do? It is quite dark and late!" asked the Kangaroo.

"You had better stay here," counselled the Wagtail. "One night more or less doesn't matter, and I don't like leaving Chip-pi-ti-chip at night-time. She likes me to sing to her all night, because she is nervous. I will go with you tomorrow morning early, if you will wait here until then."

"Having found your lost way so far!" said the Kangaroo to Dot, "it would be a pity to risk losing it again, so we had better wait for Willy Wagtail to guide us tomorrow."

To tell the truth, the Kangaroo was very glad of the excuse to keep Dot one night more before parting from her. "It will seem like losing my little Joey again, when I am once more alone," she said sadly.

"But you will never go far away," said Dot. "I should cry, if I thought you would never come to see me. You will live on our selection, won't you?"

But the Kangaroo looked very doubtful, and said that she loved Dot, but she was afraid of Humans and their dogs.

After a supper of berries and grass, Dot and the Kangaroo lay down for the night in a little bower of bushes. But they talked until very late, of how they were to manage to reach Dot's home without danger from guns and dogs. At last, when they tried to sleep, they could not do so on account of Willy Wagtail's singing to his sweetheart, "Sweet pretty creature! Sweet pretty creature!" without stopping, for more than five minutes at a time.

"I wonder Chip-pi-ti-chip doesn't get tired of that song," said Dot.

"She never does," yawned the Kangaroo, "and he never tires of singing it."

"Sweet pretty creature," sang Willy Wagtail.

# Chapter Thirteen

Two men were walking near a cottage in the winter sunlight of the early morning.

There came to the door a young woman, who looked pale and tired. She carried a bowl of milk to a little calf, and on her way back to the cottage she paused, and shading her eyes, that were red with weeping, lingered awhile, looking far and near. Then, with a sigh, she returned indoors and worked restlessly at her household duties.

"It breaks my heart to see my wife do that," said the taller man, who carried a gun. "All day long she comes out and looks for the child. One knows, now, that the poor little one can never come back to us," and as the big man spoke there was a queer choking in his voice.

The younger man did not speak, but he patted his friend's shoulder in a kindly manner, which showed that he too was very sorry.

"Even you have lost heart, Jack," said the big bushman, "but we shall find her yet; the wife shall have that comfort."

"You'll never do it now," said the young fellow with a mournful shake of the head. "There is not an inch of ground that so young a child could reach that we have not searched. The mystery is, what could have become of her?"

"That's what beats me," said the tall man, who was Dot's father. "I think of it day and all night. There is the track of the dear little mite as clear as possible for five miles, as far as the dry creek. The trackers say she rested her poor weary legs by sitting under the black-butt tree. At that point she vanishes completely. The blacks say there isn't a trace of man, or beast, beyond that place excepting the trail of a big kangaroo. As you say, it's a mystery!"

As the men walked towards the bush, close to the place where Dot had run after the hare the day she was lost, neither of them noticed the fuss and scolding made by a Willy Wagtail; although the little bird seemed likely to die of excitement.

Willy Wagtail was really saying, "Dot and her Kangaroo are coming this way. Whatever you do, don't shoot them with that gun."

Presently the young man, Jack, noticed the little bird. "What friendly little chaps those wagtails are," he said. "See how tame and fearless this one is. Upon my word, he nearly flew in your face that time!"

Dot's father did not notice the remark, for he stopped suddenly, and was peering into the bush whilst he quietly shifted his gun into position, ready to raise it and fire.

"By jove!" he said, "I saw the head of a Kangaroo a moment ago behind that iron-bark. Fancy its coming so near the house. Next time it shows, I'll get a shot at it."

Both men waited for the moment when the Kangaroo should be seen again.

The next instant the Kangaroo bounded out of the Bush into the open paddock. Swift as lightning up went the cruel gun, but, as it exploded with a terrible report, the man, Jack, struck it upwards, and the fatal bullet lodged in the branch of a tall gum-tree.

"Great Scott!" exclaimed Jack pointing at the Kangaroo.

"Dot!" cried her father, dropping his gun, and stumbling blindly forward with outstretched arms, towards his little girl, who had just tumbled out of the Kangaroo's pouch in her hurry to reach her father.

"Hoo, hoo, ho, ho, he, he, ha, ha, ha, ha!" laughed a Kookaburra on a tree, as he saw Dot clasped in her father's great strong arms, and the little face hidden in his big brown beard.

"Wife! wife!" shouted Dot's father, "Dot's come back! Dot's come back!"

"Dot's here!" yelled the young man, as he ran like mad to the house. And all the time the good Kangaroo sat up on her haunches, still panting with fear from the sound of the gun, and a little afraid

*Dot's father about to shoot the Kangaroo*

to stay, yet so interested in all the excitement and delight, that she couldn't make up her mind to hop away.

"Dadda," said Dot, "You nearly killed Dot and her Kangaroo! Oh! if you'd killed my Kangaroo, I'd never have been happy any more!"

"But I don't understand," said her father. "How did you come to be in the Kangaroo's pouch?"

"Oh! I've got lots and lots to tell you!" said Dot; "but come and stroke dear Kangaroo, who saved little Dot and brought her home."

"That I will!" said Dot's father, "and never more will I hurt a Kangaroo!"

"Nor any of the Bush creatures," said Dot. "Promise Dadda!"

"I promise," said the big man, in a queer-sounding voice, as he kissed Dot over and over again, and walked towards the frightened animal.

Dot wriggled down from her father's arms, and said to the Kangaroo, "It's all right; no one's ever going to be shot or hurt here again!" and the Kangaroo looked delighted at the good news.

"Dadda," said Dot, holding her father's hand, and, with her disengaged hand touching the Kangaroo's little paw. "This is my own dear Kangaroo." Dot's father, not knowing quite how to show his gratitude, stroked the Kangaroo's head, and said "How do you do?" which, when he came to think of it afterwards, seemed rather a foolish thing to say. But he wasn't used, like Dot, to talking to Bush creatures, and had not eaten the berries of understanding.

The Kangaroo saw that Dot's father was grateful, and so she was pleased, but she did not like to be stroked by a man who let off guns, so she was glad that Dot's mother had run to where they were standing, and was hugging and kissing the little girl, and crying all the time; for then Dot's father turned and watched his wife and child, and kept doing something to his eyes with a handkerchief, so that there was no attention to spare for Kangaroos.

The good Kangaroo, seeing how happy these people were, and knowing that her life was quite safe, wanted to peep about Dot's home and see what it was like—for kangaroos can't help being curious. So presently she quietly hopped off towards the cottage, and then a very strange thing happened. Just as the Kangaroo was wondering what the great iron tank by the kitchen door was meant for, there popped out of the open door a joey Kangaroo. Now, to human beings, all joey Kangaroos look alike, but amongst Kangaroos there are no two the same, and Dot's Kangaroo at once recognized in the little Joey her own baby Kangaroo. The Joey knew its mother directly, and, whilst Dot's Kangaroo was too astonished to move, and not being able to think, was trying to get at a conclusion why her Joey was coming out of a cottage, the little Kangaroo, with a hop-skip-and-a-jump, had landed itself comfortably in the nice pouch Dot had just vacated.

Then Dot's mother, rejoicing over the safe return of her little girl, was not more happy than the Kangaroo with her Joey once more in her pouch. With big bounds she leaped towards Dot, and the little girl suddenly looking round for her Kangaroo friend, clapped her hands with delight as she saw a little grey nose, a pair of tiny black paws, and the point of a little black tail, hanging out of the pouch that had carried her so often.

"Why!" exclaimed Dot's mother, "if she hasn't got the little Joey Jack brought me yesterday! He picked it up after a Kangaroo hunt some time ago."

"It's her Joey; her lost Joey!" cried Dot running to the Kangaroo. "Oh, dear Kangaroo, I am so glad!" she said, "for now we are all happy; as happy as can be!" Dot hugged her Kangaroo, and kissed the little Joey, and they all three talked together, so that none of them understood what the others were saying, only that they were all much pleased and delighted.

"Wife," said Dot's father, "I'll tell you what's mighty queer: our little girl is talking away to those animals, and they're all understanding one another, as if it was the most natural thing in the world to treat Kangaroos as if they were human beings!"

"I expect," said his wife, "that their feelings are not much different from ours. See how that poor animal is rejoicing in getting back its little one, just as we are over having our little Dot again."

"To think of all the poor things I have killed," said Dot's father sadly, "I'll never do it again."

"No," said his wife, "we must try and get everyone to be kind to the Bush creatures, and protect them all we can."

This book would never come to an end if it told all that passed that day. How Dot explained the wonderful power of the berries of understanding, and how she told the Kangaroos all that her parents wanted her to say on their behalf, and what kind things the Kangaroo said in return.

All day long the Kangaroo stayed near Dot's home, and the little girl persuaded her to eat bread, which she said was "most delicious, but one would get tired of it sooner than of grass".

Every effort was made by Dot and her parents to get the Kangaroo to live on their selection, so that they might protect her from harm. But she said that she liked her own free life best, only she would never go far away and would come often to see Dot. At sunset she said good-bye to Dot, a little sadly, and the child stood in the rosy light of the afterglow, waving her hand, as she saw her kind animal friend hop away and disappear into the dark shadow of the bush.

She wandered about for some time listening to the voices of birds and creatures, who came to tell her how glad everyone was that her way had been found, and that no harm was to befall them in future. The news of her safe return, and of the Kangaroo's finding her Joey, had been spread far and near, by Willy Wagtail and the Kookaburra; and she could hear the shouts of laughter from kookaburras telling the story until nearly dark.

Quite late at night she was visited by the Opossum, the Native Bear, and the Nightjar, who entered by the open window, and, sitting in the moonlight conversed about the day's events. They said that their whole rest and sleep had been disturbed by the noise and excitement of the day creatures spreading the news through the bush. The Mopoke wished to sing a sad song because Dot was feeling happy, but the Opossum warned it that it was sitting in a draught on the window sill and might spoil its beautiful voice, so it flew away and only sang in the distance. The Native Bear said that the story of Dot's return and the finding of Kangaroo's Joey was so strange that it made its head feel quite empty. The Opossum inspected everything in Dot's room, and tried to fight itself in the looking-glass. It then got the Koala to look into the mirror also, and said it would get an idea into its little empty head if it did. When the Koala had taken a timid peep at itself, the Opossum said that the Koala now had an idea of how stupid it looked, and the little bear went off to get used to having an idea in its

*Dot waving adieu to the Kangaroo*

head. The Opossum was so pleased with its spiteful joke that it hastily said good-night, and hurried away to tell it to the other possums.

Gradually the voices of the creatures outside became more and more faint and indistinct; and then Dot slept in the grey light of the dawn.

When she went out in the morning, the kookaburras were gurgling and laughing, the magpies were warbling, the parakeets made their twittering, and Willy Wagtail was most lively; but Dot was astonished to find that she could not understand what any of the creatures said, although they were all very friendly towards her. When the Kangaroo came to see her she made signs that she wanted some berries of understanding, but, strange as it may seem, the Kangaroo pretended not to understand. Dot has often wondered why the Kangaroo would not understand, but, remembering what that considerate animal had said when she first gave her the berries, she is inclined to think that the Kangaroo is afraid of her learning too much, and thereby getting indigestion. Dot and her parents have often sought for the berries, but up to now they have failed to find them. There is something very mysterious about those berries!

During that day every creature Dot had known in the bush came to see her, for they all knew that their lives were safe now, so they were not afraid. It greatly surprised Dot's parents to see such numbers of birds and animals coming around their little girl, and they thought it very pretty when in the evening a flock of Native Companions settled down and danced their graceful dance with the little girl joining in the game.

"It seems to me, wife," said Dot's father, with a glad laugh, "that the place has become a regular menagerie!"

Later on, Dot's father made a dam on a hollow piece of ground near the house, which soon became full of water, and is surrounded by beautiful willow-trees. There all the thirsty creatures come to drink in safety. And very pretty it is, to sit on the veranda of that happy home, and see Dot playing near the water surrounded by her Bush friends, who come and go as they please, and play with the little girl beside the pretty lake. And no one in all the Gabblebabble district hurts a Bush creature, because they are all called "Dot's friends".

*By the lake (evening)*

Before putting away the pen and closing the inkstand, now that Dot has said all she wishes to be recorded of her bewildering adventures, the writer would like to warn little people, that the best thing to do when one is lost in the bush, is to sit still in one place, and not to try to find one's way home at all. If Dot had done this, and had not gone off in the Kangaroo's pouch, she would have been found almost directly. As the more one tries to find one's way home, the more one gets lost, and as helpful Kangaroos like Dot's are very scarce, the best way to get found quickly is to wait in one place until the search parties find one. Don't forget this advice! And don't eat any strange berries in the bush, unless a Kangaroo brings them to you.